The air-cab rose slightly and started for the landing exit.

Glancing out a window, Monica estimated that they were about twenty stories above the street. Looking out the back window, she saw Lotus running towards them at full speed.

"Dammit!" she muttered, causing the driver to glance back at her through his rear-view mirror. It only took him a second to see the man running on the verandah after his vehicle.

"What the hell's he doing?" the driver asked.

"Just go," Monica said.

As her air-cab floated out over empty space, Lotus made a tremendous leap, landing on top of a waiting vehicle, and then another that took him sailing out towards the taxi Monica was in.

"He'll never make it," the driver said, almost in awe.

A moment later, he seemed to be proved right as Lotus — hand outstretched as he leaped towards the cab — seemed to miss it entirely as his jump came up short. He eyed Monica accusingly through the window as he began to fall.

"That's the craziest thing I've ever seen," the driver said as the cab slid into the air traffic lanes and began moving at high speed. "We must be twenty stories up. He's going to splatter like a rotten piece of fruit."

EON

The Chronos Ring Series
Eon (Chronos Ring #1)

EON

EON
Chronos Ring #1

By

Earl E. Hardman

EON

If you purchased this book without a cover, you should be aware that this book is stolen property. It was reported as "unsold and destroyed" to the publisher, and neither the author nor the publisher has received any payment for this "stripped book."

This book is a work of fiction contrived by the author, and is not meant to reflect any actual or specific person, place, action, incident or event. Any resemblance to incidents, events, actions, locales or persons, living or dead, factual or fictional, is entirely coincidental.

Copyright © 2016 by Earl E. Hardman.

Cover Design by Isikol

Edited by Faith Williams, The Atwater Group

This book is published by Vin-Vid Publishing.

All rights reserved, including the right to reproduce this book or portions thereof in any form whatsoever. For information, address Vin-Vid Publishing, P.O. Box 1586, Cypress, TX 77410.

ISBN: 978-1-937666-33-0

Printed in the U.S.A.

EON

ACKNOWLEDGMENTS

I would like to thank the following for their help with this book: GOD, who is the source of all good things in my life, and my supportive and loving family.

EON

Chapter 1

In a distant region of the cosmos, at the edge of human-occupied space, four craft dropped out of hyperspace in a brilliant, blinding burst of light. Traveling in a tight, diamond-shaped formation, the spaceships were all identical and undeniably alien in design. The vessels streaked through the void with almost purposeful determination, their destination plainly obvious: a gargantuan, circular ring made up of matching, metallic spheres.

The occupants of the ships were the Parsnaak — huge, reptilian creatures whom nature had seen fit to bless with fierce dispositions and the unrelenting desire to slay and conquer all that they encountered. The bodies of most of them bore the scars of battle — some from their enemies, but often from one another — a testament to the savage nature of their race.

The bridge of the lead spaceship was occupied by several Parsnaak, most of whom were standing at their duty stations. (Sitting on duty made one lazy and inattentive. It was a habit to be embraced by lesser, weaker species — not the Parsnaak.) Standing at the commander's terminal was General Bota, a cagey, ill-tempered veteran of numerous campaigns. His large frame brandished more marred flesh than any of his fellow Parsnaak, including a missing piece of tail and an eye that had been replaced by a cybernetic implant. Even unblemished, however, he would have cut an imposing figure.

"Helmsman," Bota said in a gruff, authoritarian voice. "Status."

EON

"Approaching the Chronos Ring," came the swift reply.

General Bota turned his attention to the viewscreen, which currently showed a line of large metal orbs ahead of them, stretching out as far as the eye could see to either side. The general knew that those spheres comprised an unimaginably colossal halo around the region of space inhabited by humans. They formed the Chronos Ring.

Bota absentmindedly growled. The Chronos Ring was the bane of his people's existence. It was all that kept them from enslaving the entire human race. They had conquered far more formidable enemies throughout their history, so the fact that *homo sapiens* had thus far been able to escape subjugation to Parsnaak rule was an injustice that rankled.

"Bring us to a halt," the general said, displeasure evident in his tone.

The lead ship quickly came to a halt, as did the other three in their convoy. The general drummed his fingers in agitation, his claws audibly clicking on the command terminal, then looked towards his first officer.

"Lieutenant Xarn," Bota said.

The lieutenant, who had been staring at the viewscreen, pivoted immediately towards his commanding officer.

"Sir?" Xarn said.

"Any sign of our 'allies'?" the general asked, uttering the last word as though it sullied him just to say it. (And perhaps it did. The Parsnaak were rumored to consider alliances as a sign of weakness.)

Xarn nodded at a young Parsnaak standing at a monitoring station.

EON

"Ensign, report," Xarn ordered.

"Scans reveal nothing," the ensign replied. "No other ships of known origin in range."

"Navigation," Xarn said, turning to another member of the bridge crew, "are we at the proper coordinates?"

The response was almost immediate. "We are in exact position."

"How long until our rendezvous?" the general asked. Xarn gave a response that was roughly the equivalent of three minutes. Not a great length of time by any stretch of the imagination, but General Bota was not known for his patience. He grunted irritably, but said nothing.

Xarn turned once again to the viewscreen, staring in almost rapt fascination at the Chronos Ring. They were probably as close as they could safely get to it; any nearer, and the Ring was likely to activate, with the spheres turning their weaponry on the Parsnaak ships. That was the Ring's purpose, after all: to protect humanity from its enemies — in particular, the Parsnaak.

To that end, the Ring was constantly in survey mode, scanning the occupants of each and all approaching vessels (and blasting into atoms those it deemed a threat). It was the Ring that had saved humanity from absolute defeat in its war with the Parsnaak, the one weapon that had finally forced Xarn's race back. Mankind may have been the enemies of the Parsnaak, but the first officer had to give them this much credit: the Chronos Ring was an engineering marvel.

From what their scientists had been able to discern, the ring wasn't a single circlet. There were at least two such bands, and they seemed to operate much like

EON

the gimbals on a gyroscope — slowly spinning in an orbital loop that encircled humanity's protected area of space, while at the same time rotating around it along some undefined axis.

"Bah, this is a waste," Bota blurted out with a scowl after about a minute, displaying the reputation he had for impatience. "This is a hoax of some sort, and I am not a humorous creature. Someone will pay for this. Turn us around; we go home."

The helmsman moved to obey. It appeared that the general was getting into one of his "moods." In any case, it would not do to get on his bad side.

"Delay the order," said Xarn, catching everyone on the bridge by surprise. It was well-known and understood that one didn't question the orders of one's commanding officer, let alone override them. Even more, doing so with General Bota was not only foolhardy, but dangerous.

The general fixed a cold stare on his first officer. Without warning, he leaped over the command podium — displaying a speed and agility that belied his age — at the same time drawing a blade from the scabbard at his waist. Faster than one would've thought possible, he had the tip of the weapon at Xarn's neck.

"Have a care when countermanding my orders, young Xarn," the general said. "I'm quite fond of you, but I've killed others who I loved for less."

Xarn was careful to make no sudden moves. "I meant no disrespect, sir, but our orders say that we wait until the rendezvous time."

It was true; their orders had come directly from the Arch-Sodal. Even a respected commander such as

EON

General Bota would be well-advised to obey, to the letter, a command from the Parsnaak ruling body.

Still, the general continued to stare at Xarn menacingly, as if he didn't care what their orders said. Then, quite unexpectedly, Bota burst into a fit of laughter. Still full of mirth, he put away his blade.

"Very well, then," the general said. "We wait."

"A wise choice, General Bota," said a disembodied voice that seemed to come from everywhere and nowhere at once.

All of a sudden, the entire bridge was on high alert. Weapons were drawn, and almost everyone was in a fighting stance. Like the rest of his crew, Bota had instinctively drawn his blade and lasergun. He looked around but could see no one.

"Who's there?" the general demanded. "Show yourself, coward."

The ethereal voice laughed. At the same time, a shimmering outline — humanoid in appearance and framed in a blue glow — slowly became visible a few feet in front of General Bota. The bridge crew, seeing the form of some creature but no physical body, stared in shock.

"What manner of being is this?" Xarn asked.

"One beyond the comprehension of your minuscule brain, soft-hide," the shimmering outline answered.

This response — to a question that was more rhetorical than sincere — enraged Xarn. However, it wasn't the taunt regarding his intelligence that galled him, but rather the last word, "soft-hide," that was the true insult. It implied that he was flaccid and weak…like a human.

EON

Furious, Xarn pulled the trigger on his already-drawn weapon, firing twice at the glistening figure. Their odd visitor took no evasive action. Much everyone's surprise, the shots passed through the glowing silhouette without hindrance. Almost immediately, there was a scream of pain on the other side of the figure, and one of the crew dropped to the floor, coughing blood and holding both hands to its abdomen, where the first officer's shots had struck.

"Put that away," the general said to Xarn, and then ordered two other bridge officers to escort the wounded crewman to the ship's medics.

"Now that we've gone through the formalities," the shimmering shape said, "perhaps we can get down to business."

"Very well," Bota said. "Why have you asked us to meet you here?"

"Because I have a bargain for you, one which I am sure you Parsnaak will find more than equitable."

"Continue."

"For several generations now, the humans have had an advanced technology that has kept them from being conquered by your fleet. I will give you the means to defeat them."

"Impossible. We have conquered worlds, entire civilizations. We have the combined genius of the best and brightest from a hundred races, and none of them have been able to match the technology the humans have imbedded in the Chronos Ring."

"Nevertheless, I will give you the means. Now, proceed forward."

"Are you mad?" Bota asked, almost in disbelief. "The Chronos Ring will destroy us."

EON

"My dear general," the voice said, laughing. "Where is your bravery? Your courage? Your faith?"

The general harrumphed. "Bravery and courage I have in ample proportions, but only a fool believes in something not tested. I've seen what the Chronos Ring can do. Your faith, then, is for the foolhardy."

"You are quite wise, General Bota," the figure conceded. "But I'm sure you didn't get that way by constantly being in the vanguard."

"Quite right," the general agreed, scratching his temple in thought. "Hmmmm."

Hit with a sudden inspiration, Bota turned to a crewman. "Ensign, get me Captain Pok on the second ship."

"Yes, sir," the ensign said. A moment later he added, "Captain Pok on the comm screen."

The image of Captain Pok appeared on the screen. Like Bota, he was a soldier who had earned his rank — mostly by dint of battle.

"Sir?" Pok said.

"Captain, I want you to attempt to pass the Chronos Ring," Bota said. "And leave your comm open."

Pok looked unsure for a moment, as if he perhaps hadn't heard the general correctly. However, he quickly recovered.

"Yes, sir," the captain said, with about as much enthusiasm as someone about to face a firing squadron. With clear reluctance, he then gave the order for his vessel to move forward. His crew seemed about as eager as the captain to obey Bota's command, but orders were orders.

"Change to exterior view," Xarn said, and the view on the comm screen changed. It now showed

EON

Captain Pok's ship breaking formation and heading towards the Chronos Ring.

General Bota and the rest of the bridge crew watched in anticipation as Pok's craft closed the distance between it and the metal spheres.

"Pok is an outstanding warrior," the general noted. "I shall not relish seeing him blown to bits."

"You worry without cause, General," the shimmering outline stated in a tone that seemed to imply boredom.

"Really?" Bota asked. "Then explain *that.*"

The general pointed to the viewscreen, which showed several of the spheres which made up the Chronos Ring opening large gunports and extending the barrels of weapons.

"Sir," said the ensign manning the comm. "Pok's ship is receiving an incoming message…from the Ring."

"On the speaker," Xarn ordered.

A moment later, a computerized voice echoed throughout the bridge.

"Attention, alien craft. You are entering an area of space under the dominion of species *homo sapiens*. Our sensors indicate the presence of a Parsnaak — a species hostile to *homo sapiens* — aboard your vessel. In addition to this, records indicate no authority for your ship to enter human-occupied space. Any attempt to come closer will be met with hostile force of an extreme nature. Attention, alien craft…"

As if the automatic warning (which kept repeating) wasn't enough, one of the spheres suddenly vanished, reappearing almost immediately next to Pok's ship, weapons ready to fire. It was a reminder that each sphere in the Chronos Ring also had its own hyperdrive.

EON

It was just another reason why the Ring was such a formidable weapon.

"They will be destroyed," Xarn said pitilessly.

"No, they will not," said their mysterious visitor. "Watch and learn."

The shimmering outline made a vague gesture, and onscreen, Pok's ship began to exhibit a blue glow. Suddenly, the message from the Chronos Ring stopped. At the same time, the weapons on the spheres withdrew. Pok's ship passed safely through and came to a stop inside the Chronos Ring.

"Unbelievable," muttered the ensign at the comm.

"Now, General," said the disembodied voice. "Send your remaining ships through."

Bota wasted no time giving the order forward, and a few moments later, all four of the Parsnaak ships were inside the Chronos Ring.

Despite the success Pok had experienced, there was a tangible sense of relief among Bota's crew — a feeling that quickly turned to elation as they realized what they had accomplished. They were the first Parsnaak in generations to enter human-occupied space.

"At last," the general said. "At last we can crush the humans."

"Sir, we should attack now," Xarn suggested. "They won't be expecting us; their defenses will be down. You'll be the hero of the ages: the Parsnaak who broke through the Chronos Ring."

"Yes, yes!" Bota exclaimed, an ambitious gleam in his eye. He was already envisioning the parade in his honor. "Prepare to attack! We'll strike before the—"

"Not so fast, General," interjected their visitor. "The bargain I made with your leaders was that I'd get

EON

your ships through the Chronos Ring. In return, the Parsnaak do a favor for me."

The general gave a dismissive wave of his hand. "We will keep our word, but Lieutenant Xarn speaks the truth. We should wage an attack now. Sitting behind their precious Chronos Ring, the humans have grown fat and weak."

"You don't want to defy me on this," the ethereal voice said in an oddly menacing tone.

"Defy *you*?!" Bota shouted, suddenly livid. "This is *my* ship! *I* give the orders." He turned to a crewman. "Ensign, tell the other ships to line up in battle formation."

Before the ensign could reply, the shimmering outline made another vague gesture. As if on cue, one of the spheres in the Ring opened a gunport and fired. One of the Parsnaak ships was hit and exploded immediately. The force of the blast rocked the three remaining ships. After a few moments, the vessels became stable again, but found themselves now manned by suddenly-somber crews.

"I will ask you again, General Bota, to remember our agreement," the bodiless voice said.

"I will remember," Bota declared. "Now, what do you require for the secret of the Ring?"

"A small thing, really," said the strange visitor. "But I now feel that some degree of insurance may be required to keep you mindful of your obligations."

General Bota was about to ask for an explanation, when suddenly another glimmering outline appeared. Unlike the first, however, this one soon took on an actual physical form. It was humanoid in appearance, but dark, huge, and impressively muscled.

EON

"This is Obsidian," the bodiless voice announced. "Obsidian, a demonstration, if you will."

Obsidian immediately dropped to one knee, and then pounded a fist down at — no, through — the solid metal floor. All around him, mouths dropped open.

"By Krako's light!" Xarn screeched.

Their odd visitor laughed. "By all means, call on your gods if you think they can help you, but let me inform you that Obsidian is an Enforcer of the highest rank. He will assist you if necessary — and ensure that you do not become forgetful of your primary mission."

"Which is?" General Bota asked.

"There is a man," the disembodied voice said. "I want you to find him and kill him."

"That would seem a simple enough task for a being of your power. Why come to us?"

"I have my reasons. You will find the man in question on the planet Muse. This is what he looks like."

The image of a man — tall and well-muscled — appeared. Young and handsome, his most striking feature was a wisp of white hair extending up from the center of his forehead into an otherwise all-dark head of hair.

"Find this man," the shimmering outline said in its strange voice. "Find him, and kill him."

EON

Chapter 2

Ian Lotus was in his apartment, slowly getting ready to attend a social function he'd prefer to skip. At the moment, he was in the process of getting dressed, languidly donning a tuxedo at a pace that would have made a sloth look speedy.

As he pulled on his shirt, he casually glanced at himself in the full-length mirror that hung on one of the walls and nodded in satisfaction. He wasn't a vain man, but he couldn't help but acknowledge (if only to himself) that he looked good: tall, dark, and handsome, as they used to say in the old days, except for a tuft of white hair at the center of his forehead. About his neck, he wore an unusual pendant — a band of gold-colored metal encircling a dark orb — but usually took care to make sure it was covered. At the moment, however, he felt it accented his wardrobe nicely.

A low ringing sound drew his attention to the comm unit, which switched on, revealing the face of a woman who was decidedly striking, despite obviously being on the verge of middle age. Behind her, Lotus could see a party of some type in full swing, with music and an excessive number of people chattering.

"You're late," the woman said.

"I know, Dionne" Lotus replied, continuing to dress.

"Look, Ian," Dionne began. "I know how you hate the spotlight, but there are a lot of important people here and I need you. The whole project needs you."

"But why?"

EON

"Because you're our best historian, researcher, and scientist. Hell, you're the most knowledgeable person we have in a dozen specialties, and you know it."

"No, I mean why are all these people here?" Lotus asked, shaking his head. "They've never shown any interest before. If we're being honest, this entire planet is just one big museum that barely gets enough tourists each year to keep the economy solvent. Why the sudden interest now?"

Dionne shrugged. "I don't know and, frankly speaking, I don't care. All I know is that we're being presented with a chance to obtain massive funds from both the public and private sectors, and I don't want to let the opportunity get away. So, as your boss, I'm directing you to be here. You have fifteen minutes, or I start docking your pay."

The comm winked out. Lotus looked at his watch.

"Shit," he muttered, noting the time, then redoubled his efforts at getting dressed.

****

Somehow, Lotus managed to finish getting attired in record time. He then hustled to his aircar, and — once it was aloft — spent the next few minutes trying to set a new airspeed record as he hustled to the main museum on the planet of Muse, where the night's festivities were being held.

Oddly enough (and much to Lotus' surprise) parking at the museum itself was fully booked — something which had never happened before. That being the case, he was forced to land at the auxiliary parking

EON

garage, then hotfoot it across the grounds to the primary building.

Determined to show up with some dignity, he slowed to a walk as he approached the front of the museum. Entering through a revolving glass door, Lotus walked briskly to the elevators at the far end of the lobby.

The museum itself was enormous in size, with a large number of exhibits. As he strode across the floor, Lotus passed an old man — elderly, but far from enfeebled. The man stared at Lotus as the younger man marched past him.

Suddenly, the elevator doors opened, and a group of people who were waiting began to file in. Lotus dismissed all thoughts of decorum and made a dash for it.

"Hold the elevator!" he shouted.

It wasn't clear that anyone heard him, because the doors began to close unabated. Just as they were about to shut completely, the doors stopped and then slid back open. Lotus stepped inside to find a lovely young woman holding the "Open Doors" button.

"Thanks," Lotus said.

"No problem," the young woman replied.

At that moment, the doors began closing again. At the same time, Lotus became aware of the elderly gentleman who he had passed.

"Gil?" the old man said, seemingly looking at Lotus. "Gil?"

Lotus reached over and pressed the "Close Doors" button, causing the doors to shut right in the face of the old man. Feeling judgmental eyes upon him as they began to move up, he turned to the woman who had held the elevator for him, truly taking note of her for the very first time.

EON

She was young — probably mid-twenties — with beautiful facial features, and dark hair tied into an intricate ponytail that dropped down just below her shoulder blades. She was dressed in an eye-catching, purple evening gown that highlighted her form perfectly. On her feet she wore an oddly distinctive pair of dark heels — the arch of the shoe curved in an unusual way.

"That wasn't very sporting of you," the woman said, clearly speaking of how Lotus had shut the elevator doors on the old man.

"It wasn't intentional," he insisted. "I guess I just hit the wrong button."

"He seemed to think he knew you."

"Unlikely," he said firmly. "By the way, my name's Ian Lotus."

He extended a hand, which the woman took as she replied, "Monica Starsong."

As they finished shaking hands, the elevator doors opened, revealing a huge reception hall. The room was full of people, both human and alien, blathering in dozens of languages. Everyone began exiting the elevator; Monica stepped slightly to the side (as did Lotus, who hoped for an opportunity to speak with her a little more), allowing the other passengers to file past her.

"Oh my," she said, looking around in surprise.

"Is something wrong?" Lotus asked.

She shook her head. "No, it's just that…I've never seen so many famous people in one place."

"Really?" Lotus raised an eyebrow as he casually surveyed the room.

Monica began pointing to various individuals. "See that man? That's Mr. Hammis — he owns mineral rights in three different systems. That woman there? She's

EON

one of the heirs to the Altair fortune. Almost everyone here is rich and famous."

"And powerful," Lotus added. "But what about you? What's your claim to fame?"

Monica lowered her eyes shyly. "I don't have one. I'm about as far as you can get from wealth and fame."

"Really?" Lotus asked, surprised. "Well, since you are a woman of limited means, please allow me to buy you a drink."

Monica smiled. "I'd like that."

The two of them began walking towards a corner of the room where a bar had been set up. However, they hadn't taken more than a few steps before Lotus felt a hand on his shoulder. He immediately turned to find Dionne standing behind him.

"There you are," Dionne said, sounding a little flustered. "It's about time. Now, come with me; there are some people I want you to meet."

"But I wa—" Lotus began.

"No 'buts,'" Dionne said flatly, cutting him off. "Now come on."

Dionne grabbed his forearm and pulled him away. Lotus looked pleadingly towards Monica, but — to his dismay — she was already talking to someone else.

Sighing, Lotus allowed himself to be dragged across the room to a small circle of men smoking pseudo-cigars. Dionne addressed the fellow who seemed to be leading the conversation — a huge bear of a man with a charismatic grin. Lotus blinked, suddenly recognizing who he was facing.

"Excuse me," Dionne said to the man, "but I'd like to introduce you to Mr. Ian Lotus. Ian is Head of Acquisitions here. He is also a top-notch historian and

EON

research scientist. Ian, this is Silas Evergreen, President of the League of Planets."

"Thanks, Dionne," Lotus said, "but I think I can recognize the current leader of the galaxy."

"Not the *entire* galaxy," President Evergreen chortled as he took Lotus' hand and pumped it vigorously. "Just the parts belonging to humanity."

"And this is Vice-President Meese," Dionne continued. "Mr. Talavisa, who owns Talavisa Shipping. Admiral Cohen, head of galactic military operations. Ambassador Gorlitz of the Neek…"

It was the start of an especially boring interlude, with Dionne making introductions to various individuals all around the room. This was the part that Lotus would have preferred to bypass — the endless line of individuals they were required to glad-hand, making nice with all of them (including the mindless, insipid ones), since you never knew who might decide to become a patron of the arts. That being the case, he initially did his best to feign excitement with each new person he met, but in short order quickly drifted back to simply shaking hands robotically while continually scanning the place for Monica.

"…and this is Ambassador Gourdatunagarbada of the Corsians." Dionne stumbled over the name of the last individual — a tall, thin humanoid creature with a gray complexion.

"I believe that's Gourdatungazada," Lotus stated, correcting her.

The ambassador looked at him in surprise. "I am impressed. The human tongue does not usually lend itself so easily to Corsian speech."

Lotus shrugged. "It's a gift."

EON

"A rare talent among those of your race," the Corsian said. "And please, call me Gourd. It is much easier to endure it in a shortened form than to hear it constantly profaned by human pronunciation."

"As you wish," Lotus replied. If either he or Dionne were offended by Gourd's words, neither showed it.

A stream of gibberish suddenly spewed forth from Gourd's mouth, causing a bewildered expression to cross Dionne's face.

"I'm Head of Acquisitions," Lotus responded absently as he suddenly spied Monica alone.

"Ian," Dionne muttered incredulously. "You speak Corsian?"

"Huh?" Lotus said, frowning as he realized he had done something irregular.

"The ambassador just spoke to you in his native language," Dionne said. "And you answered."

"Did I?" Lotus looked as surprised as his boss.

"Yes," Gourd answered. "It would seem that you have gifts that surprise even the friends who know you well."

"Well, I don't really speak Corsian," Lotus clarified. "I just catch a word here and there."

"Still, it is an accomplishment," Gourd said. "I wonder what other secrets you have hidden."

"None that I know of. Now, if you will excuse me?"

Lotus started to walk away.

"Good health to you, Ian Lotus," Gourd said to his retreating back. "And *long life*."

EON

He stressed the last two words in such a way that Lotus glanced back at him before continuing towards Monica. Seeing him approach, she smiled.

"So," she said when he got close, "how about that drink?"

EON

Chapter 3

Monica was standing alone on a balcony when Lotus came up behind her, carrying a drink in each hand. He handed one to her, then looked out over the rest of the city. They were more than sixty stories up — far from the greatest height, but tall enough to afford them a spectacular panorama. Not far from them, anti-grav vehicles zoomed by, ferrying people to and fro through the night. In the starlight, Lotus' pendant twinkled with a lively luster.

Lotus breathed deeply, taking in the view. "No matter how often I see it, I never tire of seeing the city like this."

"Is this your homeworld?" Monica asked.

Lotus laughed. "No. All those native to the planet leave as soon as they can and rarely return. The planet — and its purpose — bores them…as it does everyone else."

"I don't find it boring. In fact, it's rather nice."

"That's because you're seeing it under rare circumstances. Lots of famous people are here for a gala event. See, we recently discovered a bit of alien technology among some donated relics and we're setting up a project to research it and determine if it has any useful implications. It's gotten everyone from politicians to shipping magnates excited. In the twenty years I've been here, this is the first time that we've had so many visitors of this stature."

"Twenty years?" Monica repeated, surprised. "Aside from that streak of white, you don't look a day over thirty!"

Lotus laughed, albeit a little nervously. "You assume that I came here as an adult."

EON

"Fair enough. But weren't you bored being here with all this ancient stuff?"

"You'd be surprised by how much fun this 'ancient stuff' can be. There's plenty to keep a person occupied, young or old. This planet is a storehouse of treasure."

"Is that one of the treasures you discovered?" she asked, indicating his pendant.

"Hell no." Lotus glanced down for a second to where the ornament hung from his neck. "This is just a piece of trash I came across that someone was getting ready to toss out. I kept it because it looked interesting. As they say, one man's junk is another man's treasure. Muse has an impressive amount of items from all over the galaxy on display here, but it's nothing compared to how much is in storage or thrown away."

"Is the entire planet really just one huge museum?" Monica asked.

"Yes, that's where it gets its name: Muse. In ancient times, the Muses were believed to be goddesses who presided over the arts. They provided inspiration to poets, artists, and scientists."

"And you?" Monica said softly, leaning close to him. "What's your inspiration?"

Lotus bent his face towards hers. "I find that I'm most inspired by beauty…"

He continued leaning in her direction, as — eyes half-closed — she tilted her head up towards him. Their lips were just about to touch when a shrill scream pierced the air, coming from inside the building. Lotus, followed closely by Monica, raced back through the balcony doors.

EON

Inside, the place was filled with screams and shouts, and there was frantic motion in one area of the room. Lotus headed directly toward it.

Shoving his way through the crowd, Lotus finally made his way to the center of the commotion and stopped short. Monica, appearing without warning at his side, went bug-eyed and put a hand to her mouth in shock.

"Good Lord!" she exclaimed.

In front of them was a frightening, alien beast. For starters, it was about eight feet long and had a feline head, complete with a fang-filled mouth. In addition to a large, leonine body, the creature also had two enormous pincer-like claws, and a tail with a stinger on the end. It was held on a sturdy chain-metal leash by a slightly rotund but jovial man, who seemed to find humor in the discomfort that the animal caused the other guests.

"Scorp-lion," Lotus said, identifying the creature as he pushed Monica behind him protectively. "Stay back."

The man with the leash laughed as he tied the scorp-lion to an iron ring set in the wall.

"Not to worry," the man said. "Old Strike here is domesticated."

"I didn't know scorp-lions had been reclassified as domestic animals," Lotus said as its apparent owner walked over to where he and Monica were standing. "Does that mean you can leave your son alone to play with one without worrying about him ending up in its belly?"

The creature's owner frowned in displeasure. "I never said that. It's still dangerous to a certain extent, but the poison sack has been removed from his stinger, and

EON

we keep him so doped that he can barely walk. He's really just a walking conversation piece, and more a danger to himself that anyone around him. By the way, my name's Harlan Wreath."

"Hmmm," Lotus muttered, somewhat reluctantly shaking the hand that Wreath was now extending. "Are you *the* Harlan Wreath – the media mogul who owns the *Galaxy*?"

"Guilty as charged," Wreath said. "Assuming you mean the periodical, as opposed to the system of stars we occupy."

"You own the *Galaxy*?" Monica asked, obviously impressed. "It's one of the most widely-read dailies in…well, the galaxy."

"*The* most widely read," Wreath stated with a smile.

"So why does the owner of a newspaper have a pet scorp-lion?" she asked.

"That's one of the privileges of wealth and power," Lotus interjected. "To be able to do things that common men can't. Back on old Earth, centuries ago, the wealthy would often keep rare and dangerous animals as pets: primates, white tigers, and such."

"And the practice is still en vogue," Wreath said with a chuckle. "But as I said, Strike is harmless."

Monica glanced at the creature again. "He looks damn harmful and scary to me. Those claws look like they could crush somebody to death."

"No, not really," Wreath declared. "Their claws aren't really made to crush, just to hold their prey long enough to be stung. After that, the poison does the rest."

"Yes," Lotus said scornfully. "Yet another fine gift from the Corsians."

EON

The acid in Lotus' tone was fierce and unmistakable, causing Monica to look at him.

"What do you mean?" she asked.

"He means that scorp-lions are actually from Corsia," Wreath said. "There, they only grow to about a fourth of Strike's size and actually are kept as pets. About a hundred years ago, though, a pair escaped on a human world. The Corsians assured us that the creatures had very little adaptive capability, and most likely would die in a year or so."

"Instead," Lotus said, "they spread like rats, bred like rabbits, and thrived like roaches."

"What's a rabbit?" Monica asked.

"Never mind," Lotus said, shaking his head in disdain. "Anyway, their young are born only about the size of a fingernail, so it was easy for them to slip aboard spaceships. Now the things run rampant on dozens of worlds."

Monica frowned in thought for a second, and then snapped her fingers, clearly having a eureka moment.

"Oh yeah. I remember now," she stated. "My grandfather told me a story about one a long time ago. It was when he was a soldier on an expedition to a new world. They were camped in a forest, when suddenly a scorp-lion rushed in and grabbed a man. Somehow, the man got free and killed it. Barehanded."

Wreath nodded. "That would be Gilgamesh."

"I've heard that story before," Lotus chimed in, "and I don't believe it. I doubt if any man — even Gilgamesh — would be strong enough to kill a scorp-lion."

EON

"They say Gilgamesh was the strongest man who ever lived," Monica went on. "That he could bend metal bars with his bare hands."

"They also say he was a terrorist," Lotus added. "Don't believe everything you hear."

Practically out of nowhere, Gourd appeared next to Lotus. "You disagree with that assessment, I assume?"

"I'm probably too young to comment either way," Lotus replied.

"Then allow me to share the benefit of my experience with you," Gourd said. "Gilgamesh was a terrorist and a murderer. He killed thousands of Corsians without the slightest provocation."

"Now, now, Ambassador," Wreath interjected. "Gilgamesh may have done those things you said, but in the end his words were proven to be true: the Parsnaak received Corsian aid during their war with humanity."

Gourd casually dismissed this with a wave of his hand. "A few rogue generals can not speak for all of Corsia. Besides, they were identified and dealt with."

"And afterwards, all attacks from Gilgamesh ceased," Lotus added.

"The stories all make him sound incredible — larger than life," Monica said. "It's a shame no one knows what happened to him."

"Perhaps there are those who do," commented Gourd, casting a sidewise glance at Lotus.

"You have information that we are not privy to?" Lotus asked.

"Indeed," Gourd announced, almost smugly. "When I was made Corsia's ambassador, I took it upon myself to learn as much as possible about the human race — in particular, those events that have had the greatest

EON

effect on Corsia itself. These include both Gilgamesh and the Chronos Ring. I have found a number of interesting coincidences."

Monica and Wreath became visibly more intrigued, while Lotus fought to keep his expression passive.

"Go on," Monica said to Gourd as a small crowd began to gather around them, indicating that others had been listening to the conversation.

"Very well." The alien ambassador looked around at those gathered like a circus ringmaster. "We all know that the Chronos Ring was the product of one man — Al Chronos. The Ring protects human-occupied space from all intruders and is your first line of defense. Chronos himself is as famous as anyone who ever lived, with universities, cities, and even entire planets named after him. However, beyond his connection with the Ring, I can find no mention of him anywhere: no photographs, no images, no fingerprints, no DNA sample, no birth records, no death certificate. For a man who is credited with saving the entire human race, I find it unusual that nothing beyond a vague description of him survives."

Wreath nodded in agreement. "I have researched the subject myself, and it is well-documented that Chronos was a painfully shy man. He avoided all publicity, even going so far as to refuse to have his voice recorded."

"But you did say there was a description," Monica noted, looking towards Gourd.

"Yes, although it's not very detailed," Gourd stated. "All reports describe him as tall and well-muscled. Handsome, with a streak of white hair down the center of

EON

his forehead. He was also said to be uncommonly strong, and he wore an unusual pendant around his neck."

Gourd looked at Lotus, who merely sipped his drink, before continuing. "Gilgamesh, too, is a man of mystery. He enters the scene several years after Chronos disappears. Like Chronos, he comes from nowhere and there are no clear images of him, only a description: tall, muscular, with a streak of white hair. He, too, wears an odd pendant."

Several people, including both Monica and Wreath, followed Gourd's glance to Lotus.

"Going back even further in time," the ambassador continued, "I found even more instances of men like this, who appear at critical junctures in history and vanish without a trace. As with Chronos and the terrorist Gilgamesh, there are no means of verifying their identities."

"That's a damn shame," Lotus said, almost sarcastically.

"However," Gourd continued, as if uninterrupted, "the description is always the same."

"Don't tell me," Lotus said, laughing. "White streak of hair, muscular, strong, and with a pendant."

Monica and Wreath merely stared at Lotus. The crowd around them grew larger as more people began listening to the conversation.

"What you are suggesting is preposterous," Lotus scoffed.

"I'm afraid I have to agree," Wreath added with a nod. "Not only are you saying that the greatest hero and one of the worst terrorists in human history are the same person, but you're also suggesting that this same man has

EON

been alive for hundreds, perhaps thousands, of years. It's insane."

"Is it?" Gourd asked in a completely sincere tone. "Then allow me one last indulgence. Have you ever taken the time to ponder the names of these individuals? Al Chronos. Chronos means 'time,' and 'Al' can be seen as a mutated form of the word 'all.' Put them together, and you have 'All Time' — a fitting name for an immortal man, don't you agree?"

Monica frowned as she took this in. "Yes, but—"

"Allow me to finish," the Corsian said, cutting her off. "Next, look at the name Gilgamesh."

"Gilgamesh is generally reviled as the name of a killer," Wreath noted, "although there are some who consider him a patriot."

"That is the name as it is known today," Gourd admitted, "but in the ancient history of your homeworld, Earth, Gilgamesh was the name of a mighty king who discovered the secret of eternal life. Which finally brings us to Ian Lotus."

"Lucky me," Lotus said flatly.

As seemed to be his habit, Gourd continued speaking unabated. "The name 'Ian' could be considered a corrupted version of the word 'eon,' which is defined as an indefinite period of time. And in ancient times on Earth, some cultures considered the lotus a symbol of everlasting life. In addition to this, our good friend Mr. Lotus here has a white streak in his hair, he has an unusual pendant around his neck, and before his arrival here twenty years ago, there is no record of him anywhere."

EON

There was a deafening silence as all eyes in the immediate vicinity turned to Lotus, who suddenly burst into laughter.

"I didn't know Corsians had such a lively sense of humor," he said, "but there is no mystery in anything you've said. I'm sure if you go back far enough, there will be thousands of men to match the description of anyone living. As for the tuft of white hair, it's a fad. Look around this room — there, there, and there."

Lotus pointed to several people, all of whom had white streaks in their hair.

"Is it possible that each of them is Al Chronos and Gilgamesh as well?" he asked, eliciting a chorus of laughter from those gathered. "The pendant is a relic that I found moldering in a bin of trash that was about to be thrown out. As for names, why don't you approach President Evergreen? After all, an evergreen is a tree, and trees are symbols of long life. If he likes the joke, perhaps he won't think to be insulted by your accusations and demand a new ambassador from Corsia."

Everyone laughed uproariously at the last comment. At that moment, Lotus spied a familiar figure — the old man who had missed the elevator — entering a nearby bathroom.

"You mock me?" Gourd asked, voice full of ire. Obviously the Corsian sense of humor was less of a character trait than previously suggested.

"No," Lotus answered. "I merely make light of your outrageous suggestions. Now, if you will excuse me?"

He handed his drink to Monica, asking her to hold it for him.

"Where are you going?" she asked.

EON

"To powder my nose," Lotus replied. "I'll be right back."

EON

Chapter 4

The old man didn't seem particularly surprised when — upon exiting a bathroom stall — he found Lotus casually leaning against the wall. The elderly gentleman halted only momentarily, then continued to walk towards a nearby sink.

"Hello, Gil," the old man said as he washed his hands.

"My name's not Gil," Lotus replied.

"No?"

"It's Lotus. Ian Lotus."

"And I'm Nicodemus," the old man said. "But you already knew that, didn't you?"

"I'm sorry, but you're mistaking me for someone else."

The old man — Nicodemus — shrugged as he tapped a button near the faucet, causing the sink to now dispel disinfecting/drying solution instead of water.

"I'm old," he said. "My mind often fails me and I make mistakes. You look like a man I once knew, called Gilgamesh."

"Have you told that to anybody?" Lotus asked, standing up straight.

"I have no reason to." Nicodemus turned and eyed Lotus shrewdly. "It *is* you, isn't it, Gil?"

Lotus merely stared at him.

"I'm really surprised to see you," Nicodemus went on. "The fleet commander swore in his report that you died when your ship blew up in space. I don't know what startles me more, though. The fact that you are alive at all, or that you haven't aged a day in sixty years."

EON

Lotus ignored the comment. "What's going on, Nick?"

"What do you mean?"

"You know what I mean. Why are some of the most powerful people in known space converging on a small, backwater planet best known as a storehouse for antiquities that no one cares about? Now, you were always in the thick of things — intrigue was your middle name — so I know you've got a hand in this."

Nicodemus shook his head slowly. "No, I don't have a hand in it, but I do know what's going on. They know who you are, and they want your secret."

Lotus looked stricken for a moment, but quickly recovered. "There's no way they could know about me, or who I am. You were my closest friend and even you didn't know I was even alive until tonight."

"True," Nicodemus acknowledged with a nod, "but with you standing right here in front of me, a lot of the pieces start falling into place. And somebody knows something — why else would all these people be here?"

"I won't give it to them," Lotus insisted, crossing his arms defiantly.

"Believe me, Gil, you may not have a choice."

With that, Nicodemus walked by him and exited the bathroom.

Lotus spent a moment pondering what he'd heard, and then left as well, almost bumping into Gourd on the way out. Seeing the ambassador here was a bit of a surprise, as Corsians didn't have the same biological needs as humans.

"I must compliment you on your mental agility," Gourd said. "Despite all my evidence, you were able to reverse the crowd in your favor. I should have known you

EON

did not live so long and stay hidden so well by sheer luck. I underestimated you, but it will not happen again."

This was the last thing Lotus needed. After what Nicodemus had just shared, he had far larger concerns, and Gourd's flogging of a dead horse was starting to grate.

"Look, you have had a good jest and at my expense, but the joke's over," Lotus declared. "I like to think I'm as humorous as the next man, but a joke can go too far, and you are close to the limit."

Gourd growled deep in his throat — a perverse rumbling sound that would have frightened most people — and grabbed Lotus by the collar, pulling him close.

"You may be able to trick those other fools, but not me," the ambassador hissed. "I know who you are, and I don't care what anyone else says. You are Gilgamesh, and I'll see you punished for your crimes."

Lotus, not frightened in the least, locked onto Gourd's wrists with his hands and twisted.

The Corsian yelped slightly in both surprise and pain, letting go of Lotus' shirt. Corsians were notably stronger than humans. Few men — especially those not augmented in some way — had the strength to make him loosen his grip. He looked on in surprise as Lotus walked away.

On his part, Lotus was getting very irritated. His conversation with Nicodemus was raising some unpleasant thoughts, and running into that idiot Corsian hadn't made things any better. He was trying to figure out what to do next when Monica suddenly stepped in front of him, holding two glasses.

"There you are," she said. "I was wondering what had happened to you."

EON

"I guess I got lost on the way to the little boys' room," he stated. "That's all."

"Well, here's your drink." She reached out to hand him one of the glasses she held, but stumbled a little and ended up spilling it on his jacket.

"Oh," she exclaimed, embarrassed. "I'm so sorry."

"Don't worry about it," he said. "It's al—"

Lotus frowned and then sniffed his shirt where the drink had spilled on him. He took a deep breath and sniffed again. Suddenly, a look of shock came over his face. At the same time, an inhuman roar reverberated through the air.

Across the room, the scorp-lion let out another powerful roar, and, straining mightily, broke free of its leash. It made a beeline for Lotus; men and women scattered as it ran swiftly toward its target. One man who moved too slowly found himself gripped in its claws and thrown roughly aside, screaming in terror.

Before Lotus had time to register his surprise, the beast gripped him around the waist and slammed him into a wall, pinning him there. Fortunately, his arms were still free. The scorp-lion's stinger dove for his face. Moving almost like a contortionist, Lotus managed to twist to the side; the stinger missed him, gouging out a portion of the wall.

The stinger dove again. Incredibly, Lotus clasped his hands together and caught the tail, the stinger only inches from his face. Cords of muscle gave evidence of his strain as Lotus, with a mighty twist, snapped off the end of the monster's tail and tossed it to the floor. The scorp-lion howled, its yellow-pink blood spewing from the severed tail.

EON

While the creature was still in shock, Lotus locked his fingers together and brought them down on the joint that joined the claw to the beast's arm. There was a stomach-turning snap as the joint caved in, and Lotus dropped free. Howling in pain and rage, with one claw dangling uselessly, the beast charged him again. Lotus made a daring leap and landed on the creature's back.

Gripping its head in his hand, he twisted it to the side and pushed down, forcing the scorp-lion to the floor. Once it was down, he wrapped his legs around its neck. Then, placing one hand on its upper jaw and one hand on the lower, he pulled with all his might. The creature roared in pain; suddenly there was another sickening crunch, and the beast's body went slack.

Breathing heavily, Lotus rose from the floor, leaving the scorp-lion in its death throes.

"Incredible…" Wreath mumbled, almost under his breath.

For the first time since the scorp-lion grabbed him, Lotus looked around. All eyes were on him. Over near the elevator, he saw Monica desperately pressing the button. Full of fury, he ran towards her. Before he reached her, however, the elevator doors opened and she stepped inside. Frantically, she pressed the "Close Doors" button. The doors shut just before Lotus reached them.

"Shit," he muttered softly.

EON

Chapter 5

There were two other elevators, but Lotus quickly saw that they were both on the ground floor, and that Monica's elevator had already gone down several floors.

"Dammit!" Lotus muttered to himself. He had already inadvertently put on one show tonight; he didn't need to do so again, but he really had no choice.

He reached out and wedged his fingers between the outer elevator doors. Slowly, the doors parted as he pried them open. Inside, he could see the elevator cables, and below him the elevator itself.

Lotus looked around and snatched a tablecloth off a nearby table. He wrapped it around his hands, and then dove for the elevator cables. Gripping them in his covered hands, he slid down.

Inside the elevator, Monica heard a loud thump above her, as though something had fallen down the elevator shaft and landed on the roof of the car. She looked up for a second, and then pressed the button to let her off on the next floor.

Unexpectedly, the emergency exit in the roof opened, and Lotus peered down.

He gave her a cocksure grin, then said, "Dr. Livingston, I presume?"

A tiny lasergun suddenly appeared in Monica's hand and she fired. Lotus' face hastily disappeared from the exit, and he danced a merry jig as several laser beams shot through the roof of the elevator, which had come to a halt.

The doors opened and Monica ran out. Lotus dropped down into the elevator, bending his knees to absorb the impact, and then followed her out before the

EON

doors could close. Looking around, he found himself in what appeared to be the building's kitchen. All around him were cooks and chefs, seemingly preparing food for the party upstairs.

Monica, running ahead of him, touched a young cook on the arm and looked at him pleadingly.

"Please help me," she implored, then inclined her head towards Lotus. "He's trying to kill me."

The cook nodded, and Monica continued fleeing. Lotus, still in hot pursuit, suddenly found his path barred by not one but several of the cooks. He tried to squeeze by them, but one of them — a large, burly fellow with a heavily-tattooed face — put a hand on his chest and shoved him back.

"Please, I don't want any trouble." Lotus raised his hands up, palms open. "That woman just tried to kill a man. I have to catch her."

The cooks didn't say anything; they simply continued to give Lotus steely-eyed looks. Even worse, a number of their fellows came over and joined them, effectively surrounding Lotus.

"Okay," Lotus said, glancing around and taking stock of the situation. "We can do this the easy way, or the hard way."

Without warning, the cooks all pulled out cutting implements: knives, meat cleavers, etc.

"I guess it's the hard way," Lotus mumbled to himself, getting into a defensive martial arts stance.

****

Monica was racing down an interior stairwell when she heard a door slam from somewhere above her.

EON

Leaning over to the center of the stairwell, she looked up and saw Lotus descending the stairs. She immediately picked up the pace, running down the stairs even faster than before. Lotus, leaping down the stairs a flight at a time, quickly gained on her.

It became clear to Monica right away that she couldn't outrun her pursuer. That being the case, she took the next exit she came to. The door opened onto a long, narrow corridor; upon entering it, Monica immediately ran towards the far end.

A few seconds later, Lotus came bounding out the door. He took a moment to get his bearings, and then gave chase.

Almost without breaking stride, Monica reached down and removed a shoe. Glancing back, she threw it.

The shoe began spinning in a horizontal arc, bouncing from side to side off the walls and leaving long scars in its wake. It took Lotus a second to realize it wasn't an ordinary shoe.

What the hell? he thought as the shoe headed in his direction.

He attempted to dodge as the shoe got near him; he was mostly successful, escaping with nothing more than a small cut on his arm. The shoe ricocheted off the exit door and then flew back towards Monica. Rather than trying to dodge it, Lotus hit the deck, allowing the shoe to sail over him as it returned to its owner. Monica caught it and slipped it back on, barely slowing in the process. Lotus jumped up and resumed the chase.

The corridor ended in a T junction. Monica headed left, going out a door at the end of the passageway and finding herself on a high-level, oversized verandah that served as an air-taxi landing port. She jumped into a

EON

waiting air-cab. The driver — an overweight fellow with a long, unkempt beard — seemed surprised to find that he had a passenger.

"Uh," he began, "where to, lady?"

"Just go!" Monica screamed.

"Look lady, I can go, but you need to give me a destination," the driver insisted.

Monica leaned forward and put the lasergun to his temple. "Here's my destination."

"Oh, okay," the driver said nervously. "I know exactly where that is." The cab rose slightly and started toward the landing exit.

Glancing out a window, Monica estimated that they were about twenty stories above the street. Looking out the back window, she saw Lotus running towards them at full speed.

"Dammit!" she muttered, causing the driver to glance back at her through his rear-view mirror. It only took him a second to see the man running on the verandah after his vehicle.

"What the hell's he doing?" the driver asked.

"Just go," Monica said.

As her air-cab floated out over empty space, Lotus made a tremendous leap, landing on top of a waiting vehicle, and then another that took him sailing out towards the taxi Monica was in.

"He'll never make it," the driver said, almost in awe.

A moment later, he seemed to be proved right as Lotus — hand outstretched as he leaped towards the cab — seemed to miss it entirely as his jump came up short. He eyed Monica accusingly through the window as he began to fall.

EON

"That's the craziest thing I've ever seen," the driver said as the cab slid into the air traffic lanes and began moving at high speed. "We must be twenty stories up. He's going to splatter like a rotten piece of fruit."

Suddenly a foot shot up, cracking the glass on the driver's side window.

"Holy shit!" the driver squeaked, completely startled.

Slowly, Lotus pulled himself up until he stood on the footrail of the cab. As predicted, his leap had indeed come up short. He had almost missed the entire vehicle, but had managed to grab onto the footrail of the air-cab by his fingertips. Oddly enough, Monica, sitting in the backseat of the cab, didn't seem too surprised that he hadn't fallen.

Lotus leaned forward so that his face could be seen through the front windshield. "Take us down."

Somewhat in shock, the driver nodded and was about to comply when he felt the cool steel of Monica's gun at the back of his head.

"You might want to rethink that," she said.

Seeing this, Lotus leaned over and put one hand in front of the windshield and smacked it down, hard. With a sound like thunderclap — so loud that the cab driver jumped — the entire windshield cracked, starred so badly that the driver couldn't see.

"I have to take us down," the driver declared firmly. "We'll be killed if I try to fly like this, especially at night."

Monica howled in frustration, but put away her lasergun. As the air-cab got close to the ground, she suddenly leaped out and dashed down a darkened alley

EON

nearby. Lotus jumped down after her, the driver's shouts filling his ears.

"Hey! Who's going to pay for my taxi, huh?" the man shouted. "Who's going to pay?"

Lotus ignored him, making a dive for Monica that knocked her down. As she hit the floor of the alley, her gun skidded away. Lotus rose, and then — placing a firm grip on her upper arm — pulled Monica up roughly.

"Let me go, you psycho," she said, struggling vainly to get out of his ironclad grip. "Leave me alone."

"Right," Lotus replied. "You try to kill me, and *I'm* the bad guy."

"If I wanted you dead, I would have shoved you off the air-cab's railing. Now let me go."

"Not until you tell me who hired you."

A bewildered look flittered across Monica's face. "Who hired me? What do you mean?"

"Who hired you, who paid you, who you work for. That's what I mean."

"What are you talking about?"

"I think you know. There was scorp-bane in that drink you spilled on me. It drives scorp-lions wild, makes them crazy. I know, because I've had it spilled on me before."

"Why would I want to do that?"

"Not you; whoever's paying you. What happened up there was a test, to see what I'd do, and to find out who I was."

"Gilgamesh." Monica's eyes narrowed as she spoke the name. "You're him, aren't you?"

"I'm asking the questions here. Now, who paid you?"

EON

"I'm sorry," she stated insistently, "but I still don't know what you're talking about."

"Bullshit," Lotus declared. "You said you weren't rich or famous, but you were up there at that party. They don't let just anybody walk into those — even beautiful women — so someone must have gotten you in. Next, the shoe; that's not the kind of trick you pick up in charm school. Finally, the lasergun. It's not standard, but custom-made. No, you're working for someone, and I want to know who."

"Go to hell," she said firmly, still trying to yank herself free of the hand that held her.

Lotus sighed. "Lady, I'm trying to do you a favor here. You're in way over your head. Whatever they said, whatever promises they made, they lied."

Monica unexpectedly ceased struggling. She stared at him for a moment, then asked, "What are you talking about?"

"You know too much. I'd be surprised if you live until sunrise."

"Now you're the one who's lying."

Despite still being angry, Lotus almost laughed at the absurdity of the situation. Here he was, having his sincerity doubted by someone who had — as far as he was concerned — tried to kill him. He was about to point that fact out when he detected movement with his peripheral vision. He turned in the direction of the motion and was almost stupefied when he saw three Parsnaak soldiers step out of the shadows.

The trio wore armor and also carried laserguns. The weapons were held in their hands and at the ready, with the business ends pointed toward the two humans.

EON

"Don't move, either of you," said one of the Parsnaak, whom Lotus took to be the leader.

Monica and Lotus did as ordered, keeping quiet while — without being told — slowly raising their hands. A moment later, they found themselves flanked as the two lower-ranked Parsnaak moved next to them, one to either side. The third, the leader, stayed in front of them.

The two beside Monica and Lotus kept their weapons drawn and pointed at the two humans; lowering his gun slightly, their leader touched a button on his wrist armor and a hologram of Lotus appeared. All three of the alien soldiers seemed to study the image intently.

"Is it him?" asked the Parsnaak next to Lotus after a moment, speaking in their native language.

"I can't tell," the leader responded. "All these warm-bloods look alike to me."

While the Parsnaak talked, Monica noticed Lotus staring at the gun of the Parsnaak leader, concentrating so intently that small beads of sweat started to form near his temple.

"Well, we should kill him just to be sure," the third Parsnaak said.

"That sounds reasonable," the leader of the trio responded.

The leader's lasergun came up, but just as he was about to fire, he angled his weapon away from Lotus. The lasergun went off, striking the Parsnaak standing next to Monica. The alien soldier beside her flew backwards, a scorched hole in its chest.

The Parsnaak leader appeared shocked by his own action, clearly surprised by what had happened. Before he could recover, however, Monica — with graceful dexterity — removed her shoe and sent it flying at him.

EON

At the same time, Lotus leaped at the Parsnaak next to him.

The heel of Monica's shoe struck the Parsnaak leader right between the eyes, deeply embedding itself there. Slowly, almost leisurely, the Parsnaak's eyes rolled up into its head and it dropped to the ground, dead.

Lotus, tussling with the last remaining Parsnaak over the lasergun, suddenly dropped to the ground and rolled back, dragging his opponent down with him. Planting his feet firmly in the belly of the reptilian soldier, Lotus suddenly extended his legs, sending his adversary flying.

Lotus' actions caused his opponent to lose his grip on the lasergun. Now in sole possession of the weapon, Lotus jumped to his feet and fired at the Parsnaak, killing him.

EON

Chapter 6

Weapon still in hand, Lotus looked around to make sure there were no more assailants in the area. Convinced that no other attackers were lurking in the shadows, he relaxed. Monica, on the other hand, still seemed tense.

"Good Lord," she muttered. "Were those…"

"Parsnaak?" Lotus said when she seemed unable to finish her question. "Yeah."

He bent over to inspect the body of the Parsnaak leader. He took its armored glove off and pressed a button. The image of Lotus reappeared.

"But…how?" Monica asked, still focused on Lotus' confirmation of their attackers' identities. "How could they be Parsnaak — inside the Ring?"

"I don't know, but I'm outta here."

Lotus turned and sprinted towards the end of the alley, still carrying the glove and lasergun, which he tucked into the back of his waistband.

"Wait!" Monica yelled, retrieving her gun from the ground and then — after removing her remaining shoe — running behind him.

"What?" Lotus asked harshly when she caught up to him. "You wanted me to leave you alone, so I'm leaving you alone."

Monica looked back nervously at the Parsnaak bodies. "You said…you said I was in danger."

Lotus turned away and started walking again. At the edge of the alley he paused, and then looked suspiciously around the corner and up at the neighboring buildings.

EON

Monica, following right on his tail, stopped behind him.

"What are you looking for?" she asked, following his glance up the buildings.

Lotus didn't answer her. Instead, he ran quickly across the street to the entrance of another dark alley and started walking down it.

Monica dashed behind him.

"Aren't you going to answer me?" she asked, trailing him.

Lotus stopped and turned towards her. "Is that how it is, now? When I try to talk to you, you try to kill me. Now that you've got questions of your own, you want to be my friend."

"That's not true," she stated. "As I already mentioned, I didn't try to kill you."

"You shot at me."

Monica held up her lasergun. "This little thing barely holds a charge. I was just trying to scare you off before, keep you from chasing me. It was drained of power after the first few shots, see?"

She pointed the lasergun at a wall and fired. Much to her chagrin, a beam issued forth, ricocheting back and forth between the building walls. She and Lotus dove to the ground until the charge dissipated. A moment later, Lotus — plainly in a fury — rose up and stepped towards Monica, who was just coming to her feet.

"Sorry," she said sheepishly.

Lotus snatched the weapon from her hand, shoving it into a pocket before continuing to walk down the alley. As before, Monica followed him.

"Where are we going?" she asked after a few seconds.

EON

"Our separate ways," Lotus answered dispassionately.

"But what about me?"

"What about you?"

Monica bit her lip nervously. "Am I still in danger?"

Lotus snorted derisively. "Lady, I don't know and I don't care. We just tangled with three Parsnaak back there. Don't you know what that means? Parsnaak…inside the Chronos Ring. It's not just you and me who's in danger; it's the whole damned human race."

"So, what do we do now?"

"*We* don't do anything. *You* go back wherever the hell you came from."

Monica trembled slightly. "But…but…what if there are more of them? I'm scared to go back by myself."

"So what? You think it's safer being with me?" Lotus waved the glove in front of her face. "In case you weren't paying attention, that's my hologram they were looking at back there. The Parsnaak are looking to burn my ass, and anyone with me is going to get toasted, too."

"Is it because you're Al Chronos?" Monica asked. "Or Gilgamesh?"

Lotus' mouth dropped open, and for a second he didn't answer. Finally, he muttered, "I don't have time to go through this again. I need to get going."

"Where to?"

Lotus gave her a hard and pitiless look. "Go. Away."

"Oh please, can't I stay with you?" she implored. "Just until it feels safe again?"

EON

She gave him a beseeching look, and it appeared as though tears were welling in her eyes. Lotus tried to steel himself, but it was no use. He'd always been a sucker for a woman's tears. He sighed and shook his head in resignation.

"Fine," he said. "You can come with me until you get somewhere safe. But first, you talk. I want answers. Who hired you and why? Who's your contact? Who—"

"Whoa. One question at a time," she said, cutting him off with a wave of her hand. "For starters, I don't know who hired me. I'm a waitress at a bar, and some guy said he'd pay me to go to this party and pull a trick on his friend. All I had to do was spill a drink on somebody."

"Meaning me."

"Yeah."

"And what about the shoe, and the lasergun?"

"The shoe is easy enough. My family were circus performers for a few generations. The shoe is just one of our tricks. The gun I specifically asked for. Rich and powerful men seem to think they can get away with anything, including assault — especially when their victims are poor. I wanted some protection."

Lotus nodded in understanding. "And you don't know the guy who hired you?"

"No, he was just a barfly, like a million others," she replied. Then she frowned in concentration for a moment. "I'm curious about something. Back there when we were about to be shot, you did something. You made the Parsnaak shoot his own soldier."

Lotus shook his head, looking completely bewildered. "I don't know what you're talking about. We just got lucky."

EON

With that, he started walking towards a nearby parking garage, laboring under the assumption that he'd find suitable transportation inside that he could "borrow."

EON

Chapter 7

Lotus stopped the hovercar outside of a squalid, rundown bar. Monica eyed the building — and the surrounding area — suspiciously, and with good reason. Despite the late hour, the entire block seemed packed with unsavory characters: half-nude streetwalkers boldly strutting down the sidewalk, blatantly soliciting customers; drug runners brazenly hawking their wares; others with murder in their eyes, looking as though they'd do anything for a few credits. In short, everyone she laid eyes on looked as if they either belonged in jail, had been in jail, or had just gotten released from jail.

Lotus exited the vehicle and Monica followed his lead, getting out on the passenger side.

"Where are we?" she asked.

"The wrong side of the tracks," Lotus replied. Without closing the door, he came around to her side of the car. "Stay close, and don't talk to anybody."

"Wait," she said. "You left the door open."

"I know," he replied.

"But someone might steal the hovercar," she said, glancing around nervously.

"*I* stole it," Lotus hissed under his breath. "Or did you forget that?"

"No," Monica said, reflecting back on how her companion — saying that he didn't want his movements tracked — had casually (and expertly) picked the lock on the car they had just exited. Within seconds, he'd disengaged the alarm, and less than a minute later he'd had the vehicle started. An hour later here they were, in their current environs.

EON

"I'm thinking about us needing a way back," she continued.

"And what?" Lotus sneered. "You got moral issues with stealing a car from these decent, hard-working folk when it's time to leave?" He waved a hand in a broad, encompassing manner that took in the entire neighborhood.

Monica frowned, not sure how to respond.

"Come on," Lotus said.

He started walking without waiting to see whether she'd follow. His thoughts preoccupied by a million other things, he'd gone about half a block before he realized that Monica wasn't with him. He stopped and glanced back; Monica had barely taken a few steps from where he'd left her. She seemed to be looking at the ground and walking gingerly, one halting step at a time, as if she were in a minefield. Grunting in irritation, Lotus marched back towards her.

"What's the problem?" he demanded when he got close.

"This ground's disgusting," Monica declared almost forcefully. "I'm not going to go marching over it barefooted, picking up every communicable disease known to man."

"Barefooted?" Lotus repeated, surprised. He glanced down and saw that, sure enough, she wasn't wearing any footwear.

Of course. She'd left one shoe buried in a Parsnaak skull, and had subsequently taken off the other.

Lotus shook his head in disgust. This was exactly the kind of shit he didn't need slowing him down. Not now.

EON

"Hey honey," said a sensuous voice near Lotus' ear. He turned and found himself facing a streetwalker — a woman with skin painted flaming red, wearing nothing but knee-high boots and a see-through skirt around her waist. "Wanna get burned?"

"No, thanks," Lotus began. "I don—"

He stopped short as a thought suddenly occurred to him. He glanced at the hooker's footwear.

"The boots," Lotus said. "How much for the boots?"

The woman smiled devilishly. "You looking for a shoe-in, baby? That'll cost you extra, because of the cleaning aft—"

"No." Lotus shook his head. "The actual boots. How much?"

It took less than a minute of haggling, but on this side of town everything had a price. Shortly thereafter, Monica was sporting the boots (although she tried not to think about "shoe-ins" and the type of things her new footwear might have been used for previously). Thankfully, they were auto-fits, which readjusted to the foot size of the wearer.

She had to hustle to keep up with Lotus, who had a long stride and had started walking the second she had the boots on. He was clearly a man on a mission.

"So, where are we going?" she asked, sounding a little winded as she cantered along beside Lotus.

He gave her a sideways glance. For a second it seemed that he was going to ignore her, and then he responded.

"Maxima's," he said flatly — as if that explained everything.

EON

Monica found his answer unsatisfactory, but held her tongue. Two blocks later, they reached their destination: a beat-up, three-story building centrally located in a notorious red-light district, as evidenced by the large number of porn shops, prostitutes (and clientele), and overall graffiti plastered everywhere.

"Here we are," Lotus said, pointing at a flashing neon sign that advertised the name of the edifice they stood in front of as "Maxima's." (It came as somewhat less than a surprise to Monica that the actual name on the sign was "*Cli*-Maxima's," but someone had smashed the first three letters.)

"A brothel?" Monica said. "What are we doing here?"

Lotus smiled. "If you have to ask that…"

Leaving the rest unsaid, he slipped past a man and cybernetic woman haggling over the price of something called a "metalstorm" and went inside.

Looking a little nervous and hesitating only a moment, Monica followed.

The interior was only slightly less of an eyesore than the outside. The walls could use a new coat of paint, the carpet was worn in a number of spots, and the various pieces of furniture — based on the acts she saw people engaged in on them — probably needed to be burned. That, combined with the snippets of conversations she overheard as she and Lotus headed towards a bar near the far wall, gave the place an overall sense of smuttiness that was almost palpable.

"Hey," Lotus said, attempting to get the bartender's attention.

EON

The bartender — a huge, hulking female who was obviously on some massive steroid regimen — turned to Lotus.

"No outside vaj," the bartender said in a gruff voice as she tilted her chin towards Monica.

"Hey!" Monica screeched, obviously offended at being taken for a lady of the evening. "I'm not a hoo—"

"That's fine," Lotus interjected. "I'm looking for Maxi."

The bartender harrumphed. "The boss lady don't come cheap — and threesomes up the ante." She gave Monica a frank stare. "You sure you can afford it?"

Lotus laughed. "Just tell Maxi that Ian Lotus is here."

The bartender shrugged. "Okay, but it's your funeral if you ain't got the scratch. Boss lady don't like having her time wasted." She leaned in conspiratorially, whispering, "Don't take it personal if she asks me to bust you up."

"Not a chance," Lotus said nonchalantly, causing the bartender to eye him warily as she stepped away.

"Who's Maxi?" Monica asked.

"Hmm?" Lotus mumbled, lost in thought. "Uh, the owner."

"And just how is it that you happen to know the owner of a brothel?"

"Oh, well, that's a long story," Lotus began. "Suffice it to sa—"

"How much?" said a gravelly voice next to Lotus. Glancing to where it came from, he saw a tall, thin man with an oversized, bulbous head. The fellow had rough-looking skin that was purple-brown in color, and elongated arms that went down to his knees. Noting

EON

suction cups on the man's hands, Lotus recognized him as an *octo hominid* — a genetically engineered person made by splicing human DNA with that of an octopus.

"How much?" the octo asked again.

"I'm not interested," Lotus replied.

"How much for *woman*?" the octo clarified testily, holding up cash in its suckered fist and nodding towards Monica (who looked horrified at what was being suggested).

"She's not interested either," Lotus said flatly, trying to inconspicuously slide into a fighting stance. Octos were notably fast and notoriously strong, but had extremely poor vision — a fact he'd use to his advantage if this situation escalated (as it seemed on the verge of doing).

"This is Maxima's," the man declared fervently. "*All* is for sale."

"Not tonight, friend," Lotus stated. "Move along."

Rather than heed that advice, the octo flung the money it held in Lotus' face, shouting, "You take cash! I take girl!"

The man moved deliberately towards Monica, apparently considering the issue settled. Lotus, placing a firm hand on the fellow's shoulder, spun him around and then threw a punch at the man's face. Faster than seemed possible, the man's hand came up, catching Lotus' fist before the blow could land. Undaunted, Lotus tried to strike a blow with his free hand, only to be met with the same result.

The octo wriggled the digits of his hands, and suddenly the fingers of the two combatants were interlocked. The suckers on the man's hands attached

EON

themselves painfully to Lotus' palms, who merely grunted in response.

Lotus swung his hands outward in a circle, and then brought them in, wrists up, between himself and his opponent. Following this maneuver, he lifted upwards, trying to bend the octo's arms at the wrist. Normally, this would have had the effect of forcing an opponent to painfully yield in lieu of having some bones broken. However, the octo wasn't built like a normal human being; the man's arms seemed completely flexible, like the tentacles of an octopus.

The man grinned, and then began asserting the same upward pressure that Lotus had tried to use on him, bending Lotus' wrists painfully. The octo basically expected to break his adversary's wrists and then take the woman. That's why, clearly accustomed to being the stronger opponent when in a fight, he couldn't hide his surprise when Lotus not only resisted the force he was applying, but actually began to reverse it.

Unexpectedly, Lotus swung his arms outward, then immediately jumped up, kicking the octo in the face. There was a satisfying crunch as his foot connected, and as his legs came down, Lotus happily noted that blood was gushing from his adversary's nose. The man seemed dazed; not wanting to give him time to recover, Lotus jumped up and kicked him again. This time when his feet came down, the octo was plainly wobbling. Without warning, the octo's eyes rolled up in his head. As he fell backwards, unconscious, the suckers released their grip on Lotus' hands with a staccato-like series of pops.

Lotus turned to Monica, who had watched the entire encounter in horrified fascination. He was about to

EON

ask her whether she was alright when a voice cut across the atmosphere of the bar like a knife.

"Ian Lotus, please tell me you're not crippling my patrons again."

Lotus swung around to face the direction the voice had come from. Approaching him was a statuesque woman, completely bald but with exquisite facial features. Her near-perfect body was clothed in nothing but a sheer white gown that hid absolutely nothing, was obviously inadequate for keeping out the cold, and served no purpose that he could discern other than being something that could be seductively removed — or ripped off — later.

"Hello, Maxi," Lotus said, leaning forward to give her a kiss on the cheek.

"Well?" Maxi gestured towards the unconscious octo.

"Oh, he wasn't a patron," Lotus stated. "At least not of *your* place."

He cut his eyes to Monica; Maxi followed his glance, but declined to comment further on the subject.

"Since I haven't seen you in a decade, I can only assume this isn't a social call," Maxi said. "What do you need?"

"My room," Lotus said.

Maxi gave him a gorgeous smile. "Certainly. And since you asked for me, I assume I am to join you." She gave Monica a sly wink. "That being the case, we can use my chambers, although I must warn you, Ian, this isn't like the old days. I don't give freebies any—"

Lotus cleared his throat, interrupting Maxi while avoiding Monica's judgmental stare. "No, not *a* room. *My* room."

EON

Maxi frowned for a second, as if unsure of what Lotus had said. Then, understanding seemed to dawn on her, and she softly muttered, "Oh."

EON

Chapter 8

Lotus' "room" turned out to be a sparsely furnished, one-bedroom apartment located in a corner of the sub-basement under Maxima's. The entry was located behind a stack of boxes and crates that it had taken several minutes to move, and Maxi had also had to retrieve a special set of keys to unlock the door. She'd stayed only a moment after opening the door and letting them in.

"It's been ten years," Maxi had said, glancing around what was seemingly the living room, "but I trust you'll find all is as you left it." And with that — after soliciting a promise from Lotus that he'd lock up when he left — she had placed the keys in his hand and departed.

Almost immediately thereafter, Lotus had locked the door and then headed to the bedroom. Monica walked in slowly behind him, watching nervously as Lotus took off his jacket and tossed it onto a nearby chair, then removed his tie and began to unbutton his collar.

"Look, I don't want you to think I'm ungrateful for everything you've done tonight," she said from the doorway, "but I'm not ready to repay—"

"Calm down, princess," Lotus said as he rolled up his sleeves. "No one has designs on you — at least not anymore and not down here. You can plan on leaving here with your maidenhood intact."

Without another word he turned and, gripping one end of the bed, lifted and moved it aside. The bed had been resting on a large carpet, which covered a good portion of the floor. Now that the bed had been moved aside, she could see that the carpet contained an image of a couple copulating — something that (like the mirrored

EON

ceiling above them) should not have come as a surprise given their current locale.

"Is this really your place?" Monica asked.

"Yep," Lotus answered, lifting up one end of the carpet and pulling it back, revealing a tiled floor underneath.

"But Maxi said you haven't been here in ten years."

"Obviously I don't *live* here." Lotus dropped to his knees. "I did Maxi a favor years back. She offered to thank me in her own special way, but I asked for the room instead."

"I get it. This is some kind of safe house — a retreat in case anyone ever found out who you were."

On his hands and knees, Lotus appeared to be searching the floor for something. "Bully for you, Sherlock. You figured it out. You win a Kewpie doll."

"What's a Kewpie doll?"

Lotus ignored her, continuing to seemingly feel around the floor.

"What are you looking for?" Monica asked.

Lotus was tempted to say that he'd lost a contact lens, but that would just invite further inane questions.

"Do you need some help?" she asked, hiking up her dress and getting down on her knees as well. Rather than answer, Lotus simply held up a hand in a "stop/stay back" type of gesture.

Monica sat back on her haunches, looking a little lost.

"Well, the place is certainly clean," she noted, glancing around.

EON

Lotus sighed. His failure to engage wasn't shutting her up, but maybe he could at least guide the direction of the conversation.

"There's a robotic cleaning unit in one of the closets," he said, responding to her last statement and nodding towards a door in the bedroom wall. "It comes out once a month and cleans the place, then plugs back into its charging unit. There!"

That last word was plainly not related to the conversation they were having, and as Monica watched, a section of the floor dropped down a few inches and then slid to the side, revealing a rectangular opening about three square feet in size.

Of course — this was some kind of floor safe, Monica now realized. Lotus hadn't simply been fumbling around on the floor; he had been pressing tiles in a specific pattern in order to unlock it.

As she watched, he pulled a metal box out of the opening by an attached handle, then stood and retreated to the other room. She got up and followed him, noting that the door to the floor safe was now sliding back into its original position.

Flopping down on a sofa in the living room, Lotus placed the metal container on a coffee table in front of him and opened it. Inside was what looked like the myriad pieces of some kind of electronic device or apparatus: wires, diodes, a miniature receiving dish, and more.

As Monica watched, Lotus carefully removed the items from the box. She sat down on the couch next to him.

"Can I help?" she asked.

"No," he said firmly. "You'll only get in the way."

EON

Folding her arms, Monica sat back in a huff and watched Lotus work.

****

Ten minutes later, an odd little contraption sat on the coffee table. It looked like a cross between a tiny submarine and an oscilloscope, with the tiny receiving dish spinning on top and odd symbols scrolling up on a small screen.

"What is that?" Monica asked as Lotus fiddled with the device.

"I suppose you could call it a diagnostic tool," Lotus said.

"For what?"

Lotus hesitated for just a moment before answering. "The Ring."

Monica almost went bug-eyed. "Really? What's it saying?"

"The Ring is still functional, if that's what you're wondering. I can't really tell much more than that, though — certainly not how Parsnaak soldiers entered human space. The signal's too weak."

"It's not strong enough to diagnose the problem? Then what good is it?"

"Hey," Lotus uttered defensively, "the problem is that we're pretty far away and there's too much interference. There's a lot more crap obstructing the signal than when I set this up — satellites, communication relays, and so on."

"I suppose it's hard to keep up with the times with an elongated lifespan."

EON

Lotus gave her a very hard stare, then whipped out the Parsnaak lasergun. For a moment, Monica thought he was going to shoot her, but he fired instead at the contraption he had just built. Sparks flew from it, and then it melted down into a pile of slag.

"Come with me," he said, heading to the bedroom. Meekly, Monica stood up and followed him.

Inside, Lotus was standing with the closet door open. He pulled down a clear, sealed package.

"Put this on," he said, tossing the package to her.

Through the transparent covering, Monica could see that it contained some casual women's clothing. A second later, Lotus pulled down another similar pack, obviously containing clothes for himself. He turned to find Monica staring at him in an odd way.

"What's the problem now?" he asked.

Monica glanced at the package, and then at her companion. She bit her lip nervously, as if afraid to speak.

"I can't change with you standing there," she said. "I ne—"

"Oh, give it a rest!" Lotus fiercely shouted. "I've seen plenty of tits in my life, and from where I stand, yours are nothing special. And if I'm that eager to see a pair, I could just go upstairs. Now hurry up; you're wasting time."

With that, he marched out of the bedroom and slammed the door.

Monica hurriedly climbed out of her dress. Opening the package, she pulled out a pair of dark pants and a light blue shirt. A minute later, she was fully dressed.

Inspecting herself as best she could in the mirrored ceiling, she then stepped towards the bedroom

EON

door. She was about to open it when she realized that — after professing modesty and wanting to change in private — she should give Lotus the same courtesy. She gently knocked on the door.

"Hey, are you decent out there?" she asked.

There was no response, even after she waited for a few seconds.

"Hey," she said, raising her voice and knocking even louder. "Is it okay to come out?"

Silence. Monica was preparing to knock a third time, when the truth dawned on her. Yanking open the door, she raced into the other room. Lotus' tuxedo shirt and pants were on the sofa, but the man himself was nowhere to be seen.

That asshole, she thought.

EON

Chapter 9

Lotus tried to maintain a cool and calm demeanor as he negotiated with the ship captain. It wouldn't do to seem too eager to leave Muse — that would only jack up the price. The fact that he was arranging transport on a freighter rather than a passenger ship was suspicious enough and had already cost him double the normal fare. (The captain, a man by the name of Etienne, wasn't really buying Lotus' story about feeling passenger ships were too crowded.) He didn't want to overpay for the additional element of discretion.

Not that money was a problem; he had access to a number of healthy bank accounts. He'd also had plenty in the apartment beneath Maxima's, and had surreptitiously slipped a few wads of cash into his pocket from the closet while digging around in there for clothes. Then, while Monica had been changing outfits, he had swiftly donned new garments himself and left. He'd left word with Maxima to make sure Monica got home — wherever that was — safe and sound.

The distinct tinkle of a glass breaking — having fallen from a waitress' tray — brought Lotus back to himself. Still, it took him a moment to remember where he was: at a booth in the back room of a bar, negotiating with the captain of a freighter.

"Booking passage is one thing," the captain was saying in an effort to wring more money from his prospective passenger. "Keeping your name off logs and manifests is something else."

The man then proceeded to list the number of people (primarily crew) who would have to be bribed to look the other way if Lotus truly wanted to maintain

EON

anonymity during the voyage. When Captain Etienne finally got down to the numbers, he actually named an initial price that Lotus would have been happy to pay. However, not wanting to appear overeager (or too flush with cash), Lotus haggled until the price was cut in half.

Satisfied, the captain finished his drink and stood. "Be at the dock in two hours."

"Understood," Lotus said. Captain Etienne gave him a curt nod and then left.

Alone now, Lotus took a sip from his own drink — a blue concoction with a generous amount of fizz but very little alcohol. He wouldn't have been averse to something a little stronger, but he needed to stay sharp for the nonce.

Two hours to kill.

He was just giving some thought to how he should spend that time when someone slid into the seat across from him that the captain had recently vacated.

It was Monica.

"You're really not a nice guy, are you?" she asked, although it was really more of a statement. "Deserting me in a brothel?"

Lotus stared at her in frank surprise for a moment before finding his tongue. "How did you find me?"

"I think I deserve an answer to *my* question first," she said.

"Listen, lady," Lotus practically hissed. "We're not together. We're not partners. We're not some team jointly working towards a common goal. You're a stray that I picked up and has now taken to following me around. So I'm asking again, how did you find me?"

Monica, looking a little hurt by his words, lowered her eyes. "We're too far away," she said softly.

EON

Lotus shook his head in confusion. "What?"

"Back in that basement room, you said we were too far away from the Ring. That implied that we — *you* — needed to get closer. That means leaving the planet."

"And you knew that this area was one of the prime hangouts for space crews."

"*Everybody* knows that," she corrected. "So if you were trying to ship out and lie low, I knew you'd be somewhere around here."

"Bravo." He clapped his hands softly. "That's good deductive reasoning. But it just begs the question: why are you here?"

"I was hoping that…" Monica looked down momentarily and twirled her thumbs nervously. "I was hoping that I could come with you."

A short laugh burst out from Lotus. "Ha! That's unlikely."

"Please. This place is a dead end. I need to get off this rock."

"And you think it's a good idea to come with me?"

She frowned. "Why wouldn't it be?"

"Have you forgotten about the Parsnaak? That they're on my ass?"

"All the more reason for you to have someone with you."

Lotus leaned back and shook his head. "I'm sorry, but I can't be responsible for you. Plus, I'm not sure I trust you."

"Fine," she said with a slightly bitter tone. "How about a trade then?"

Lotus laughed again. "What could you possibly have that I'd want?"

EON

"Can't you guess?" She gave him an odd look.

He looked her up and down. "We were just in a brothel, where I could have had a world-class sample of the one thing that you *might* have worth trading. Obviously, I'm not interested."

"No," she said in an exasperated tone. "Not *that*."

"What then?"

"I'll take you to the guy who hired me to spill the drink on you."

Lotus leaned forward, suddenly interested. "I thought you said you didn't know him."

"I don't. But I've seen him and can point him out to you."

"What?" Lotus muttered, unable to keep the surprise out of his voice. "Here?"

"First, your agreement. I point him out to you, and you take me with you when you leave."

Lotus hesitated a moment. His instincts were telling him this was all wrong. However, he was currently in the dark about a lot of things: the Parsnaak hunting him, the possible failure of the Chronos Ring, being set up to be lunch for an alien beast... This was possibly a chance to shed some light on at least one of those issues.

"Fine," he said, coming to a decision. He gulped down the rest of his drink and stood up. "Now, take me to this 'friend' who wanted to play a joke on me."

"He's right over there," Monica said, pointing.

Lotus looked in the direction indicated, his eyes settling on a table currently occupied by four large, sinister-looking individuals. He didn't recognize any of them.

"Which one?" Lotus asked.

"The one with the metal arm," she replied.

EON

Lotus eyed the man she referred to, noting that he was a cyborg. There was no telling how much more of him was artificial, but with that arm he was going to be at least as strong as the octo Lotus had faced at Maxima's.

Oh well…

Lotus sauntered over to the table in question. As he walked, he mentally sized up the men at the table. Aside from the cyborg, at least one of the other men was augmented in some way, as evidenced by his eyes (which were completely silver in color). The remaining two men seemed normal, for lack of a better term.

Conversation between the four men came to a halt as Lotus' approach made it clear that he was headed to them. He stopped about a foot from the table and just stood there, silently glancing at each of those seated in turn. It didn't take long for the silence to become uncomfortable.

"Can we help you, friend?" asked the cyborg, in a tone that didn't sound friendly in the least.

"I hear you're looking for me," Lotus replied.

The cyborg looked genuinely surprised. "Excuse me?"

"You've been looking for me," Lotus repeated.

The cyborg shook his head. "You're confused, pal. I've never seen you before."

"Likewise," Lotus responded. "But it wouldn't be the first time someone I hadn't met tried to do me in."

"Do you in?" The cyborg frowned. "Look, I don't know what your problem is, but you're about to have a bigger one."

As he spoke, the cyborg came to his feet (as did his companions); he stood a good head taller than Lotus, who — despite appearing to be at a disadvantage

EON

physically and numerically — did not give the impression of being intimidated. In fact, Lotus seemed not to have noticed that the encounter had apparently escalated. He was busy looking around for Monica; he was getting the impression that the cyborg was being sincere, and wanted her to verify that this was indeed the man who had hired her.

"Hey!" the cyborg shouted. "I'm talking to you!" With his metal arm, the man grabbed Lotus by the neck and hoisted him off the ground.

Lotus brought his hands up and got a grip on his assailant's wrist with both of them. At the same time, almost like an acrobat, he lifted his legs and locked his feet behind the man's head. Then he flung his body in a twisting motion.

The angle and momentum of Lotus' spin forced the cyborg's head down while simultaneously causing the man to loosen his grip on Lotus' neck. Keeping his hold on his opponent's wrist, Lotus unlocked his feet and landed lithely on the floor. He then delivered a savage kick to the cyborg's exposed rib cage.

With the average person, Lotus actions would have at least fractured some ribs, if not shattered them. The cyborg, however, only took a few shambling steps back, indicating that his metallic parts included more than just his arm. He rubbed the spot where he'd been kicked gingerly, and then smiled. At the same time, his three companions moved to surround Lotus.

"That's enough of that," a firm voice announced. Lotus glanced around to find a squad of soldiers marching in, weapons drawn. They surrounded him and the four men he'd been about to fight; all five of them

EON

silently raised their hands in the air, as the other patrons in the bar began to inconspicuously leave.

One of the soldiers wore the rank of major, and had apparently been the one who had spoken.

"As interesting as it would be to let this little scenario play out," said the major, "my orders are to make…sure…nothing…"

The major's voice trailed off and he seemed to be staring at something over Lotus' shoulder — an area where Lotus could see the beginnings of a strange sound-and-light show with his peripheral vision. Before he could turn in that direction, there was a brilliant flash that made almost everyone in the bar close their eyes reflexively in response to the brightness.

Lotus' vision cleared a moment later, and when he looked at the area that had been the origin of the illumination, he saw something that made him blink.

A colossus stood there, humanoid in appearance but taller even than the cyborg — heavily muscled, and built in such a way that he instinctively knew that its hide was armored. Something about it set off alarm bells in his brain, as if the thing radiated menace. As if to confirm this suspicion, he heard a voice at the same time, firm yet ethereal, like something out of a dream but only in his head.

"Obsidian," the voice said. "*Kill.*"

The colossus — Obsidian — went into motion, heading straight for Lotus. In its path was the cyborg; the man threw a punch with his metal arm, a powerful blow that would have crushed the skull of most men. Obsidian caught it in his fist, and then squeezed; sparks flew as the metal fist was pulverized. Obsidian, moving incredibly fast for one so large, released the fist and then —

EON

grabbing the cyborg by the shoulder — ripped the metal arm clean off.

Wailing in anguish, the cyborg flopped to the floor, screaming.

Sensing movement from the soldiers and instinctively knowing what was about to happen, Lotus dropped to the ground as gunfire erupted. The soldiers had opened fire without anyone giving the order to do so. Frankly speaking, no one had to. It was inherently obvious that Obsidian — whoever and whatever he was, wherever he had come from — plainly represented a distinct and undeniable threat.

As Lotus had suspected, the gunfire appeared to have no discernable effect on the colossus, which stepped forward and reached for him. Almost in a panic, Lotus immediately rolled away, angling so as to bring himself out of the line of fire. The second he was clear, he leaped to his feet.

Obsidian was directly in front of the soldiers now. Unaffected by the hail of gunfire, he grabbed one of them by the waist and flung him aside; the soldier hit the wall and went through it with a bone-shattering smack.

"Obsidian!" shouted the dreamlike voice. "Remember your task!"

The gargantuan figure turned towards Lotus, who was eagerly looking for a way out. The front door was currently occupied by the soldiers. There was a nearby passage that led to a back exit, but going for it would take him pretty close to Obsidian, who had already shown he was faster than he looked and was now headed in Lotus' direction.

All of a sudden, an odd cylindrical object landed at the feet of the colossus. Lotus took one look at it and

EON

dove for a nearby table, gripping it as he slid across its surface and thereby making it tilt over as he slid off it. In short, it acted as a barrier as the object he had seen — a grenade — went off. Shrapnel and debris went flying; Lotus, as far as he could tell at the moment, was unhurt. Obsidian, too, seemed to have escaped injury, but the explosive had returned his attention to the soldiers, who continued firing at him without effect.

Realizing that his team was seriously overmatched, the major screamed, "Retreat!"

It wasn't clear whether everyone heard him; some of the soldiers immediately turned and ran, while others — perhaps in a foolhardy attempt at glory — stood their ground and continued to fire. They quickly learned their lesson as Obsidian grabbed another of their fellows and tore him in half at the waist. After that, they were all fleeing.

Looking to take advantage of the situation, Lotus scrambled to his feet and made at dash for the passage leading to the rear exit. At the same time, he saw more grenades being tossed. He was down the passage and halfway to the exit when the first of the grenades went off.

EON

Chapter 10

Lotus awoke on his back with a loud and annoying ringing in his ears. He seemed to be covered with dust, rubble, and rubbish. He sat up and the world spun crazily. Still, he was able to figure out where he was: outside the rear exit of the bar where he'd booked passage with Etienne, although he couldn't remember much after that. Something seemed odd about the place, and when he looked again, he realized that not only had the back door been blown off the bar, but there was also a huge hole in the wall.

Lotus struggled to his feet, wobbling from dizziness. There was something important he had to do…something he needed to remember. Around him, others were running amok — some shouting, some screaming. Everyone appeared to be in distress. He took a few halting steps and then stopped, his head spinning so wildly that he couldn't get his body coordinated. He would have collapsed then, if not for someone putting his arm around their shoulder and holding him up.

He looked towards the person, eager to thank them, then frowned as he saw who it was:

That woman who had started his night going downhill. *Monica.*

She said something he couldn't understand, but heard himself mumbling back a response of some sort. He began to say something else to her as well, something critical, but before he could get a grip on what it was, everything went dark.

****

EON

Lotus awoke with a start on a firm but comfortable mattress, then scrambled to his feet as he realized he wasn't in his own bed. Through his toes, he felt a familiar vibration — a minute quivering that was indicative of large machinery rumbling somewhere nearby. He was on a spaceship.

"Well, look who's finally awake," said a woman's voice.

Glancing in the direction of the voice, he saw Monica seated in a nearby chair with a blanket over her. She had obviously just woken up herself — probably roused by him jumping out of bed.

"Where are we?" he asked.

"On your friend Captain Etienne's ship."

"How'd we get here?"

"By the skin of our teeth," she answered with a grin. When Lotus seemed unimpressed by her humor, the smile faded and she went on. "While you went to speak to the guy who hired me, I went to the ladies' room — down the hallway near the exit. When I came out, I could hear gunfire, so I ran out the back."

"So you didn't try to see what was going on?"

"I wasn't interested in getting my head blown off, if that's what you mean."

"So you don't know what happened to the big guy who showed up out of nowhere?"

Monica gave him a queer look that made it clear that she didn't know what he was talking about and shook her head. "The only thing I saw was you getting blown out the back like a rag doll a short time later. I went to help you and mentioned taking you to a doctor. You said not to — that I should bring you to Etienne's ship."

EON

"So you did."

"Yes. Now do you see why it's good to have someone watching your back? By the way, the captain says you owe him extra for my fare."

Lotus ignored her last comment. Taking stock of himself, he suddenly realized that he was still covered with enough dust to be considered grimy.

"I need to take a shower," he announced.

"Right in there." Monica pointed to a doorway which, Lotus now noticed, appeared to lead to an interconnected bathroom. Without another word, he headed in that direction.

Although not huge, the bathroom did contain all the basic necessities (toilet, sink, etc.), plus an insta-laundry machine. Lotus removed all the items from his pockets — cash, the Parsnaak glove, weapons, and so on — and placed them on the counter next to the sink. Next, he stripped down, tossing all his clothing into the insta-laundry. Finally, he stepped into the frameless shower and turned the water on high, both in terms of pressure and heat.

For a few minutes, he did nothing but stand there, letting the water cascade over him, washing away the grime while kneading the tension from his muscles. Before long, the entire bathroom was thick with steam.

Without warning, there was an audible click as the bathroom door opened. Lotus was instantly on high alert. He narrowed his eyes, but couldn't see through the steam.

Dammit! he thought, realizing that he'd left the weapons he'd been carrying on the sink. He could see a form moving towards him through the vapor and tensed, ready to go on the offensive.

EON

"It's just me," said Monica, and Lotus relaxed as she stepped closer, her features becoming visible.

"What are you doing in here?" he asked.

"Since you're injured, I thought you might need someone to wash your back," she said. "Or any other hard-to-reach areas."

"No…" Lotus began, then realized that she was disrobing. "Um, maybe."

A moment later, completely nude, she stepped into the shower with him.

"I thought you were shy," he said.

"No, I'm modest. There's a difference."

"Which is?"

"Shy would mean I'm timid or frightened easily. Modest just means I have regard for some aspects of common decency."

"I see. And I guess it wouldn't be decent to let an injured man try to shower himself."

"Not at all."

With that, she reached towards a soap dispenser set in the shower wall. She pressed a button, and a moment later liquid soap shot into her waiting palm. She rubbed her hands together to create a thick lather, and then rubbed it on Lotus' chest.

On his part, Lotus hadn't moved. Moreover, as much as he tried not to, he couldn't resist letting his eyes wander all over Monica's gorgeous frame. What was worse, the more he tried to avert his eyes, the more they kept coming back to her, settling on her hips, her thighs, her breasts…

As he feared, it wasn't long before she noticed the extra attention he was giving her. Slyly noting his attempts to steal glances at her, she flirtatiously placed a finger to her jawline, and then seductively traced an invisible line with it down her neckline, to her chest, down the center of her bosom, watching his eyes follow all the while.

"Still think you've seen better?" she asked in a honeyed voice as her finger traced the curve of her right breast.

"I could be induced to revise my initial assessment," he said, then he leaned in and kissed her.

EON

Chapter 11

"Wakey, wakey," said a stony voice that Lotus didn't recognize. At the same time, he felt something cold and hard being pressed against his forehead. He opened his eyes to find, as he expected, a gun aimed at him.

The man holding the gun was slim and middle-aged, with a balding pate and a scraggly beard. There was also a younger man, stout and with innumerable piercings in his eyebrows, ears, and other body parts — including a bull ring through his nose.

Both men were dressed as members of the ship's crew. Monica wasn't in the bed with him (which was where he'd last seen her before falling asleep), and Lotus was on the verge of asking about her when he thought it better to keep silent. She might be hiding somewhere in the room rather than having been taken away, as he had initially assumed. Taking a quick peek to the side, he noted that the bathroom door was closed.

"What's this about?" Lotus asked.

"I believe we're at your stop," the older man said. "This is where you get off."

"We're supposed to be headed to LeGrande," Lotus said, naming the planet he'd booked passage to. "There's no way we've been traveling long enough to get there yet."

"We got a smart one, here," said the younger man, laughing. "Bet your mum's proud."

"So is this how your captain does business?" Lotus asked. "Dumping passengers into the void in the middle of a trip?"

"Oh, you've misjudged us, son," the older man said, motioning with the weapon for Lotus to get out of bed. "You're not getting voided. You're being transferred."

"Yeah." His companion chortled. "You've got another ride, that's all."

"So why the gun?" Lotus asked as he stood up.

"Just to make sure you don't give us any trouble," the younger crewman said. "And to make sure you turn over any valuables to us."

"For safekeeping, I suppose," Lotus said sarcastically.

"Exactly," said the older man.

All of a sudden, the door to the bathroom swung open. The older man shifted his weapon in that direction, apparently ready to fire. Monica stood there, naked.

Seeing her like that caused a delayed reaction on the part of the crewmen. Lotus, taking advantage of the distraction she'd provided, reached over and gripped the older man's gun hand. He slammed it against the wall, making the man yelp in pain and drop the gun. Lotus then brought up a knee, landing it squarely in his opponent's belly and knocking the wind out of him. Finally, he threw a punch that connected solidly with the man's jaw, whipping it to the side. The fellow dropped to the floor, unconscious.

At the same time, Lotus heard gunfire behind him, followed by the sound of a body hitting the floor. He turned to find Monica in a firing stance, holding the gun he'd placed on the bathroom counter. On the floor in front of her was the other crewman. A neat hole had been scorched through his upper right shoulder from laser fire, and a large knot was beginning to form on his head.

EON

"Are you okay?" Lotus asked, coming over to check on her.

"I'm fine," she replied. She nodded at the crewman in front of her. "He tried to rush me, so I shot him in the shoulder. As he was going down, he hit his head on the chair."

Lotus nodded in approval. "Good job."

****

Captain Etienne's ship was of a design that Lotus knew well. Thus, he and Monica were able to make their way to the bridge without incident, needing to hide themselves from approaching members of the crew only twice. Needless to say, it came as quite the surprise to the captain and the other half-dozen members of the crew who were present when their two passengers walked onto the bridge with weapons at the ready.

At the time, there was a voice coming through the comm channels, indicating that Etienne had been in the process of speaking to someone. Lotus raised a finger to his lips, indicating silence, as he approached the communications station. He flipped a switch on the communications relay, essentially muting all conversation in the room with respect to anyone on the other end of the comm channel.

"Etienne, stay where you are," Lotus commanded. "The rest of you, against the far wall."

Hands raised, the bridge crew did as ordered, and Lotus left them under Monica's watchful eye, ordering her to shoot anyone who so much as twitched. Then he turned to the captain.

"So who are we talking to?" Lotus asked.

EON

"Some admiral in the Space Navy," Etienne replied. "He's got a small convoy of ships out there."

Lotus raised an eyebrow. "An admiral, huh? What's he want?"

"Just listen."

Keeping his weapon trained on the captain, Lotus listened to what the speaker was saying on the comm channel.

" —peat it again," the voice said authoritatively, and with a little hint of impatience. "We have no interest in impounding your decrepit vessel, arresting your criminal crew on the many outstanding warrants they have, or impounding any of the shitty cargo we know you're smuggling. We only want your passenger."

"What have you said to him?" Lotus asked.

"What do you think?" the captain responded. "I told him we'd hand you over."

"Tell him again," Lotus ordered, before taking them off mute.

"I've already told you," Etienne said loudly, "my men are getting him. We'll put him on a lifeboat and you can have him. But as I've mentioned, the lifeboats weren't properly prepped prior to departure. You've got to give me time to make sure it's functioning properly, or he'll be dead — from asphyxiation, depressurization, or a million other things — before he gets to you."

The voice on the other end of the comm unit laughed derisively. "You mean give you time to get your smuggled goods off it. Fine — you've got ten minutes. Like I said, we don't care about the cargo you're hauling."

Lotus turned the mute button back on. "Is that true, about smuggled goods being on your lifeboats?"

The captain nodded. "Yes."

EON

"And how does the smuggling work, exactly?"
"Well, it all depends…"

****

Lotus and Monica were in one of the lifeboats, tuned in to the open comm channel between the bridge of Etienne's ship and the unknown admiral.

"Okay," Etienne said. "Your man's on board the lifeboat, along with the woman he brought with him."

"Woman?" the admiral said, seemingly confused. "What woman?"

"They're disengaging now," the captain said, ignoring the admiral's question.

The transfer tube, through which they had walked in order to board the vessel, began to withdraw, retreating back to the main ship. At the same time, the clamps holding the lifeboat in place opened, releasing the craft from their grip.

"Etienne, you're not answering me," the admiral said. "What woman are you talking about?"

"You should be able to pick them up on your sensors momentarily," the captain stated. "Right now they're close to our hyperdrives, so you may have trouble getting an accurate read with your scanners."

"Ignoring me would be a big mistake, Etienne," the admiral said. "Now tell me about this woman!"

"Sir," said a barely audible voice, apparently one of the admiral's crewman. "I'm detecting an odd energy signature."

"What kind of signature, Ensign?" asked the admiral.

"Just give it a minute," Captain Etienne said.

EON

"It's rather muffled," the ensign said, "and it looks like there's interference from their engines, but it looks like a separate hyperdrive."

"A separate…" the admiral began, then began shouting. "Stop them, dammit! It's a tri—"

Lotus didn't hear anything else as the lifeboat made the jump to hyperspace.

EON

Chapter 12

Lotus had to admit that Etienne's smuggling operation had some of the hallmarks of genius. Rather than personally dropping off and picking up illicit goods, the good captain retrieved and delivered via a lifeboat with preloaded coordinates. (Of course, this system only worked with known, trusted associates and clients. For others, personal pick-up and delivery was still a necessity.)

After explaining how his system worked (including how his ship's hyperdrive engines could mask that of the lifeboat), the captain wasn't particularly adverse to Lotus' plan — namely, that Lotus and his companion use the lifeboat to make their escape. Etienne had little love for government forces like the Navy, and he was even more averse to being shot (which was a likely outcome if he didn't help Lotus.) And so he had allowed his voice to be recorded and then had put up little fuss as he and his crew were locked in the brig of their own ship.

Monica was almost giddy with excitement at their narrow escape from naval forces. Lotus was more circumspect, and began plotting their next jump almost the second they dropped out of hyperspace.

"We're leaving?" she asked after Lotus told her not to get too comfortable. "But we just arrived, and I thought LeGrande was our destination anyway." She looked out the observation window at the planet below them, a greenish-white orb floating in space.

"No. LeGrande was just a way station, a place where we were going to change ships," Lotus corrected as he fiddled with the navigation system. "Besides, the Space Navy won't have any problems getting info from Etienne about where we were headed. Their forces will be on their way, if they aren't here already."

"So where are we going?"

"Our real destination — at least for this leg of the journey."

"Which is?"

"New Onyx."

EON

Chapter 13

Contrary to what the name implied, little about New Onyx was contemporary or modern. Everything from the architecture to the fashions were, in Monica's opinion, outdated by decades, if not centuries.

Upon arriving, Lotus had immediately taken them planetside and docked the lifeboat. He had then given Monica some cash and asked her to get them a room somewhere while he took care of some other business. She had balked at the idea; he had already tried to leave her behind once and she didn't doubt his willingness to do it again.

"Great," said Lotus, after she explained her position. "So you're going to make us waste twice as much time by doing everything together rather than splitting chores down the middle."

"Like you said, we're not partners," she noted. "In fact, I'm not sure what we are."

Lotus stared at her for a moment, then threw up his hands. "Fine. Come along if that's what you want."

From the spaceport, they took an air-cab to a nearby city, getting out at a midlist hotel. After obtaining a room there (which Lotus didn't even deign to visit before leaving), they took another taxi to one of the larger downtown buildings, which housed a large and venerable interplanetary bank.

"What's in here?" Monica asked as they went inside.

"Money," Lotus said snarkily. "That's what most banks have inside."

"But that's not why we're here, I assume."

EON

Lotus sighed in exasperation. "No, we're here for something else."

They were in the lobby. Most of the customers present were being assisted by virtual tellers. Against a far wall was a row of offices, each of which seemed to be occupied by an actual person who was present in the flesh. That said, some of those they were assisting appeared to be holograms.

"Come on," Lotus said, and began walking towards the offices. There were perhaps ten of them, and he headed for the first one in which the occupant did not seem to be waiting on a customer.

The bank officer in question was a handsome woman who was probably just entering middle age. She wore a custom-made pants suit, and had her hair done up in a large bun. She sat behind her desk, busy staring at a computer screen, but looked up when Lotus knocked and entered (without waiting to be invited), followed by Monica.

The woman, whose nameplate identified her as Yulia Zsa Zsa, gave them a severe look as they came in. The way her eyes darted about their persons, it was clear that she was weighing them in some judgmental capacity — and that they had been found wanting.

"Can I help you?" she asked, stressing the question in a way that made it obvious that she didn't plan to be helpful at all.

"Yes," Lotus said as he and Monica sat down in a couple of chairs that faced the bank officer. "I'm here to withdr—"

"Any of the virtual tellers can help you make withdrawals," the woman announced dismissively, cutting

EON

him off and already turning her attention back to her computer.

Lotus cleared his throat. "Thanks, but I'm afraid I really need to speak with an officer."

The woman let out an exasperated sigh. "I'm afraid, sir, that the personal services of officers for this branch are restricted to clientele who meet very specific and rigid account requirements."

"I see," Lotus said, seeming to ponder what she had said. "Well, can I just give you my account information and you can tell me which teller I should see?"

"I can assure you, sir, they're all the same."

"Please," Monica interjected, giving the woman an imploring look. "It will help us get out of here that much quicker."

The bank officer seemed to mull that statement over, and then muttered, "Alright, although this is highly irregular…"

She tapped some keys on her computer and then asked for the specific account number in question. Lotus rattled off a series of numbers, digits, and special characters that seemed to go on for five minutes. When he finished, the bank officer hit the submit button on her computer — and then did a double take. Her mouth dropped open, and she stared at Lotus as if he had a penis growing out of his forehead.

"Sir!" she practically screeched, coming to her feet. "I'm so sorry, sir! I didn't realize you had an Apex Account!"

"Oh?" Lotus remarked casually. "Did I fail to mention that?"

EON

****

For the next two hours, bank officers tripped over themselves trying to wait on Lotus and Monica. They hadn't had an Apex Account member physically present in decades. In fact, they made such a fuss over him that Lotus had a tough time getting them to acknowledge his reason for being there: that he wanted to retrieve some possessions from their vault.

Eventually, Lotus and Monica were taken by special elevator deep underground. There followed a long series of checks and verifications to confirm that he was indeed the owner of the account, including retinal scans, fingerprints, and voice identification. Lotus passed all such tests easily. The only odd incident occurred when one of the examiners noted that the retinal patterns on file for Lotus' account were over a hundred years old.

Lotus had made no comment about it, and when he glanced at Monica (who, as the guest of an Apex member, was busy enjoying a massage at the time), she didn't appear to have overheard the statement. (In Lotus' opinion, she was far too busy marveling over the perks of Apex membership, such as the fact that they were even allowed to hang on to their weapons.)

In the end, they were shown to a vault that required a special code to be entered — not just by Lotus but also by two bank officers (one of whom was Yulia Zsa Zsa) — in order to unlock. At that juncture, they were left alone. Only then did Lotus swing the vault door open and step inside.

The interior, Monica noted, was a small room about one hundred square feet in size. On the floor in the center of the room was a metal box similar to what had been in the floor safe in the room beneath Maxima's.

"Alright," Lotus said, picking the box up by the handle. "We're done here."

EON

Chapter 14

They left the bank and returned immediately to the hotel, where they finally got a chance to visit their room. Monica, understanding that Lotus had booked them a suite, was eager to get inside. Lotus, however, had become exponentially more wary since retrieving the mysterious box from the vault. (He had spent the entire ride from the bank constantly looking behind them, as if they were being followed.)

After unlocking the door, Lotus entered the darkened suite ahead of Monica, with the lasergun ready.

"Lights on," Monica said, earning her an evil look from Lotus (who had apparently expected her to stay silent for the nonce).

The lights automatically came on, revealing a nicely furnished living room, with two glass doors leading out to a balcony. There was a kitchenette which contained a small breakfast table. Floor-to-ceiling mirrors on one wall gave the impression that the room was much larger than it actually was. Another door on the opposite wall seemingly led to the bedroom.

Methodically, Lotus began to go through every room, closet, and corner while Monica watched him with a bemused look on her face.

"What are you looking for?" she asked rhetorically. "There's no one here. No one knows that we're even on this planet."

Lotus ignored her until he completed his inspection of the premises. Finally satisfied that they were truly alone, he came back to the kitchenette and took a seat at the breakfast table, placing the metal box in front of him. As before, he opened it up and began taking out various pieces of equipment.

"What's all this?" Monica asked. "Another diagnostic device?"

Lotus hesitated, and for a moment it seemed that he wasn't going to reply. Then he said, "Not exactly. This is part of a device that modifies the parameters of the Chronos Ring."

"Modify…" she repeated. "You mean like change it?"

"Yeah. The fact that we've got Parsnaak within human-occupied space means that something's happened to the Ring, and I need what's in this box to fix it."

"Can you do it now? From here?"

"I can do it from just about anywhere if all the parts are properly assembled."

"Are you about to do it now?"

"No," he said, stifling a yawn. "I'm a little tired and there's a chance I could screw something up."

"In that case," she said, slinking off towards the bedroom in a sultry manner, "I'm going to take a shower. Feel free to join me."

It took nary a second for Lotus to get up from the table and follow her.

****

Monica rolled over in her sleep and reached for Lotus, coming somewhat awake when her hand closed on empty sheets. She sat up and looked around. The room was dark, as was the adjoining bathroom where they'd had their second shower together. However, light showed around the base of the bedroom door, indicating that he was probably out in the living room. At least she hoped he was... Not caring to be deserted a second time, she tossed on her clothes and then raced from the bedroom.

To her relief, Lotus was there, already dressed and sitting at the breakfast table, working on his contraption. He looked up as she came in and gave her a bright smile.

"Surprised to see me?" he asked, obviously aware of her concern.

"Surprised to see you *awake*," she clarified. "It's still hours before dawn."

"Yeah, well, I woke up and couldn't go back to sleep. Rather than just lie there for hours, I decided to do something productive."

"How's it coming?" she asked, eyeing the device that he was putting together.

"It's a little more complicated than the previous one, so it's taking a little longer."

Monica was about to say something else when an odd beeping noise began. Both she and Lotus looked at each other, perplexed.

"What the hell is that?" he asked, rising to his feet.

"Sounds like some kind of alarm," she replied. She followed the noise to the bedroom, which seemed to be where it was originating. When she opened the door, she was surprised to not only hear a beeping (which had increased in tempo), but it was also accompanied by a red flashing light. The source of both disturbances seemed to be something on the nightstand by the bed.

Brusquely and without apologizing, Lotus swept past her and into the room. He grabbed the flashing object and brought it into the living room. Now that she could see it clearly, Monica realized it was the Parsnaak

EON

glove — the one that had projected the hologram of Lotus back on Muse.

Without warning, the pace of the beeping and flashing increased again. And again. And again.

Monica frowned, nonplussed. "What in the world…?"

Suddenly Lotus' eyes went wide as the truth dawned on him.

"Oh shit…" he muttered, and then raced for the balcony doors. Frantically, he opened them, stepped out on the balcony, and flung the glove away.

"Down!" he screamed as he dashed back inside, grabbing Monica and pulling her down behind the sofa. They had just hit the floor when a powerful explosion shook the entire building, sending shattered glass and debris flying into the hotel room.

Rising from the floor, Lotus checked to make sure Monica was alright, and then — after being assured that she was — went to survey the damage.

The glass from the balcony doors was almost completely gone. Stepping outside, he saw a huge hole blasted in the building next door. The railing for their balcony had been warped by the blast in a major way, but was still mostly intact.

"Whoa. That was way too close." Monica said, stepping out beside him and looking around. "So all the time you were carrying that glove around, you didn't know it was a bomb?"

"That wasn't standard issue the last time we faced the Parsnaak," Lotus said defensively. "They've obviously upped their game since the last time we met."

"Regardless, I think I've had enough excitement for one night."

EON

Lotus pointed up. "Don't bet on it."

Squinting, Monica looked in the direction he was indicating. At first she couldn't see anything, and then she gasped, placing a hand to her mouth.

Out of the night sky, a trio of air-cycles — each ridden by a Parsnaak — swooped down towards them. Laserguns mounted on the air-cycles began to fire at Monica and Lotus, who raced back inside amidst laser blasts. Simultaneously, they both dove for cover behind the couch.

"Lights off!" Lotus shouted.

The lights went off just as the three air-cycles drew to a stop, hovering just beyond the balcony. The three riders immediately began to fire inside, weaving from side to side.

Streaks of light filled the apartment as the lasers shredded almost everything in sight. A comm unit exploded as it was hit. Holes appeared in the walls, exposing electrical wires which began smoldering. A cabinet in the kitchenette was sliced open, and pots and pans poured out.

After a minute or so, the Parsnaak stopped shooting. They lowered their air-cycles to the balcony and got off. The apartment at this point was filled with smoke and debris. The Parsnaak had their laserguns out and ready as they walked through the place.

Still crouching behind the couch, Lotus gave his lasergun to Monica.

"Here," he said as she took the weapon. "Try to draw their fire."

"What are you going to do?" she asked.

"Try not to get killed, for starters."

EON

Lotus scuttled away into the smoke-filled room and was soon hidden from view. The three Parsnaak fanned out, plainly looking for their quarry. Monica, peeking around the edge of the couch, found her eyes irritated by the smoke.

Lotus, huddled in a corner, watched a Parsnaak approaching his hiding spot.

Come on…come on, he said to himself. *Fire, you stupid girl, fire.*

Monica rubbed her eyes vigorously and blinked almost spasmodically in an effort to see.

Lotus watched nervously as the Parsnaak got closer.

Come on…now or never, he thought.

Suddenly, as if she heard his silent appeal, Monica began to fire. The Parsnaak near Lotus, like the other two, turned in her direction and prepared to shoot. Lotus quickly rose up behind the reptilian soldier and placed a hand over his mouth. Dropping his weapon, the Parsnaak reached up with the intent to pull Lotus' hand away, but was unable to accomplish any such thing before Lotus snapped his neck. In its death throes, the Parsnaak kicked away the weapon it had dropped. Frustrated, Lotus lowered the body gently to the floor.

The other two Parsnaak, caught in the open, fired as they dove for shelter. While they were preoccupied with trying to hit Monica, Lotus began sneaking up on another of them.

Without warning, Monica stopped firing. Hearing her struggling with the weapon, Lotus realized that her gun was jammed.

One of the Parsnaak looked up to see Lotus almost on top of him. Thinking he had an easy kill, the

EON

soldier fired at point-blank range. Unfortunately, what he fired at was actually Lotus' reflection in a large mirror against one wall. The laser fire ricocheted right back at him, striking his weapon and making it explode in his hands. The Parsnaak collapsed to the ground and didn't move.

The third Parsnaak took a shot at Lotus, who dove aside and disappeared into the haze. Listening intently, the Parsnaak heard Monica desperately trying to unjam her weapon. Chuckling, the Parsnaak rose up and fired short, controlled bursts, calmly walking over to Monica's position.

On her part, Monica curled into a ball, trying to make herself as small as possible while the shots zinged through the couch.

Suddenly the laser fire stopped; Monica looked up to see the third Parsnaak standing over her, preparing to fire. Unexpectedly, a white cloud appeared around him, accompanied by the hiss of air escaping from a pressurized container. The Parsnaak dropped his weapon and screamed as Lotus, holding a fire extinguisher, continued to douse the reptilian soldier with its contents. He didn't stop until the Parsnaak was on the floor, unconscious.

"Lights on," Lotus said. Despite the room being shredded by gunfire, the lights flickered crazily for a second — as if debating the request — and then turned on.

Lotus tossed the fire extinguisher aside as Monica stood up, staring at the last Parsnaak.

"What did you do to it?" she asked.

"Damn thing's cold-blooded," he answered. "Too much cold on them is as good as a laser."

EON

She pointed to the fire extinguisher. "Where'd you get that thing?"

"I found it when I searched the place earlier." He knelt down beside the Parsnaak and felt for a pulse.

"Is it dead?" Monica asked.

Lotus shook his head. "No, just knocked out."

Glancing around, he spied a tall, metal lamp lying on the floor. Propping the Parsnaak up, Lotus took the lamp and, straining, bent it around the reptilian. Monica watched in open-mouthed surprise as he used the lamp to pin the Parsnaak's arms.

"Holy shit," she said. "You're strong as…I mean, you really are Gilgamesh. And Al Chronos."

Lotus ignored the comment. In the distance, he could hear sirens approaching. "We don't have much time, and I need answers."

He slapped the Parsnaak and shook it.

"Hey, Sleeping Beauty," Lotus continued. "Wake up."

"Who's Sleeping Beauty?" Monica asked.

Ignoring her, Lotus slapped the Parsnaak again, and it growled softly in response.

Lotus drew back his hand for another slap. "I said wa—"

A noise behind him caused Lotus to turn around. Monica stared as well as a thin vertical line of light appeared from nowhere on the other side of the room.

"Holy…" Monica began, then stopped as her voice froze in her throat.

A huge foot stepped out of the light, followed by the equally elephantine body of Obsidian.

EON

Lotus stared for a moment, and then picked up the third Parsnaak's lasergun and pointed it at Obsidian in one fluid motion.

"Hold it right there, friend," Lotus warned, "unless you want a ventilation problem with your chest."

He was halfway bluffing. He assumed this was the same brute he'd seen in the bar on Muse, and if so, Lotus had seen it withstand laser fire before. However, that had been with human weapons; he now held a Parsnaak weapon of a decidedly higher caliber. Maybe it could do some damage.

Obsidian ignored him and took a ponderous step forward.

"I'm warning you…" Lotus continued.

Obsidian took another step and Lotus fired. Obsidian jerked slightly (indicating that the Parsnaak weapon could possibly hurt him) and a wisp of smoke rose from where the laser made contact, but he kept walking forward.

Lotus stared in surprise before firing again. The second shot was as ineffective as the first.

"Obsidian," said a voice that Lotus heard only in his head — the same voice he'd heard in the bar back on Muse. "Kill."

Lotus let the Parsnaak slump back to the floor, forgotten. As Obsidian closed in on him, Lotus backed away, still firing.

Obsidian ignored the shots as Lotus fetched up against the wall. Towering over Lotus, Obsidian snatched the lasergun from Lotus' hand. Lotus watched in disbelief as the colossus put the metal barrel of the gun into his mouth and bit it off.

EON

Lotus jumped up and landed a kick directly on his opponent's face; Obsidian barely moved. Lotus then landed a solid punch to Obsidian's midsection, only to clutch his hand in pain a second later.

Obsidian dropped the lasergun and hit Lotus with a backhand that sent him flying across the room. The giant then stalked over towards Lotus, who was slow getting up.

Monica, forgotten by the two fighters, grabbed a metal frying pan and ran behind Obsidian. She smashed it against the back of his head with all her might. Obsidian, almost on top of Lotus, suddenly stopped. Slowly he turned to face her, and then simply stood there.

Monica took advantage of the opportunity to whack him again, this time in the face. The pan came away with Obsidian's features imbedded in it. Monica stared at it in shock.

"Oh shit," she muttered, realizing that she was in serious trouble. She looked at Obsidian pleadingly. "You wouldn't hit a lady, would you?"

Obsidian's answer was a slap that sent her flying out towards the balcony, where the three air-cycles still hovered. She groggily tried to get back to her feet.

Obsidian turned his attention back to Lotus. Grabbing him around the throat with one hand, Obsidian lifted him from the floor. Lotus heard his bones start to creak under the pressure of Obsidian's grip. Out of the corner of his eye, he saw Monica get on one of the air-cycles and take off.

You bitch... he thought.

Suddenly, Obsidian noticed the pendant around Lotus' neck. The giant wrapped his free hand around it, only to be greeted by a shocking wave of electricity.

EON

Obsidian grunted in pain as the shock coursed through his body. His grip on Lotus loosened, and both collapsed to the floor.

Lotus, gasping and on his knees, massaged his neck. Unbelievably, Obsidian began to rise. Lotus, too weak to move, watched helplessly as his adversary came at him.

Suddenly, Monica came streaking through the shattered balcony doors on the air-cycle.

"Incoming!" she shouted.

She aimed the cycle right at Obsidian, but jumped off just before the moment of impact. The air-cycle struck Obsidian at full speed, driving him through a nearby wall. Monica got up and raced over to Lotus.

"You okay?" she asked.

"Oh yeah," he replied, sounding winded. "I enjoy being throttled."

Monica helped him to his feet. "Guess you thought I left you, huh?"

"The thought had occurred to me," Lotus said as she guided him over to one of the remaining air-cycles.

"Well, never let it be said that Little Nica deserts her friends," she said, making Lotus think she was taking a subtle jab at him. "I had to build up some speed to knock your sweetheart off his feet. By the way, what was it you did to him back there?"

"Ancient Chinese secret," Lotus mumbled.

Monica looked at him oddly, but didn't respond. She helped Lotus onto one of the two remaining cycles, then got on the same one in front of him.

"You'd better fly with me," she said by way of explanation. "You're not looking too good."

"Whatever," said Lotus, still massaging his throat.

EON

As they prepared to take off, a queer noise sounded behind them. Glancing back, they both saw Obsidian coming back through the wall, pushing the air-cycle in front of him.

Down by her foot, Monica noticed a discarded lasergun. Getting a toe under it, she flicked it up into the air, and then caught and fired it with uncanny dexterity. Her shot struck the air-cycle Obsidian was pushing, exploding it as their own cycle rose up higher.

Lotus looked at her in surprise. "I take it that's another trick you learned on the family farm."

Monica merely laughed. She flipped the lasergun over her shoulder to Lotus, who expertly caught it.

"You'd be surprised at the tricks I've learned," she said over her shoulder. "I could show you a thing or two."

"I don't believe it," Lotus muttered.

Monica grinned. "Is that a challenge? I like challenges."

"No, I mean I don't believe it. Look."

Monica glanced behind her, and her mouth almost dropped open. Standing on the ruined balcony, his clothing in tatters, was Obsidian.

"Who is this guy?" Monica asked.

"I believe his name is Obsidian," Lotus said. "But that's all I know."

She turned their vehicle to face him just as Obsidian grabbed the remaining air-cycle, which was still on the balcony, and flung it at them.

Monica quickly and deftly scooted them to the side, and Obsidian's makeshift missile flew past harmlessly. It slammed into the building behind them and exploded. Monica raised her middle finger to Obsidian.

EON

"You missed us, dipshit!" she shouted.

She turned their air-cycle around and zoomed away just as Obsidian leaped. He grabbed onto the edge of the craft, metal crunching in his grip as the air-cycle wobbled. Lotus looked around to see what had thrown them off-balance, and was utterly amazed to see Obsidian dangling behind them.

"We've got company," Lotus whispered in Monica's ear.

She looked back and saw Obsidian.

"Hang on," she said. "It's gonna be a bumpy ride."

With that, she let the air-cycle go up to full throttle and took off. In an effort to shake Obsidian off, Monica began to fly in a manner that, in Lotus' mind, could mildly be dubbed as suicidal — for example, taking extremely sharp turns between buildings and flying so close to skyscrapers that Obsidian brushed against them, tearing loose bricks. Her antics kept their unwanted passenger off-balance enough that he couldn't do much more than hang on, but it also became clear that he wasn't going anywhere.

"Keep going," Lotus said as an idea suddenly occurred to him. "I'm going to try something."

Still holding the lasergun in one hand, Lotus spun around to face the rear and kicked out, trying to stomp Obsidian's fingers. He connected, but only succeeded in hurting his foot.

Taking a calculated risk, he tried to get closer in order to kick the colossus in the face. It was a nigh-fatal error, as Obsidian's hand suddenly reached out and brushed his leg aside.

EON

Lotus was dislodged from his seat and almost thrown from the cycle altogether, but managed to hang on using his free hand. However, both he and Obsidian now dangled from the craft. Obsidian reached for him, but Lotus contorted his body crazily and avoided being grabbed. Obsidian tried to catch him again, but an insane dive by Monica made the giant miss (although Lotus was barely able to hang on).

"Hey!" Lotus shouted. "Are you just trying to kill him or both of us?"

Obsidian reached for Lotus a third time and grabbed him by the shirt. Desperate, Lotus fired the gun not at Obsidian's hand, but at the metal portion of the cycle that the colossus had gripped. The metal gave and Obsidian fell away, ripping Lotus' shirt in the process. Lotus let the lasergun drop and, using both hands, regained his seat. However, the air-cycle began to bob and dip wildly.

"You can stop the crazy driving now," Lotus said to Monica. "He's gone."

"Yeah, well, so's the stabilizer," she declared. "What the hell happened?"

"Uh…he broke it off when he fell."

"Well, we're gonna have to go down. I can't control this thing much longer."

Lotus raised an eyebrow in surprise. "Doesn't feel like you're controlling it now."

"I'm not. It's stopped responding."

The wall of a building loomed ahead of them. At their rate of speed, they'd be smashed like bugs.

"Well, you need to do *some*thing," Lotus insisted. "And fast."

EON

"I can't do anything," she said. "I can't control it. We're going to crash, so you better hang on to something."

They both closed their eyes and braced for impact as the air-cycle headed for the side of the building. Nothing happened. After a second, they opened their eyes.

Their air-cycle had stopped mere inches from the wall, but they and the vehicle were bathed in a white light.

"What happened?" Monica asked.

"Tractor beam," Lotus answered.

He looked up toward the origin of the beam and saw a huge spaceship above them. Slowly, they rose up to it.

"We're being reeled in," Lotus stated.

"By who?" Monica asked.

"I wish I knew."

EON

Chapter 15

Aboard the ship, Monica and Lotus found themselves escorted down a long hallway, surrounded by guards.

"Where are they taking us?" Monica asked softly.

"I don't know," Lotus answered, "but we may have been safer with the Parsnaak."

"I doubt that. At least these guys are human."

They entered a large room with a huge conference table. Seated around the table were a number of individuals that Lotus recognized, including Nicodemus, Ambassador Gourd, and Wreath, the media mogul. Only two chairs at the table were empty. A large number of comm screens were mounted on the walls.

Without warning, one of the guards sprayed a mist in Lotus' face that sent him into a fit of coughing.

Nicodemus got up and helped him into one of the empty chairs; Monica sat in the other.

"Sorry about that, Gil," Nicodemus said, "but you'll understand the reason for it in a minute."

"Told you…" Lotus gasped loudly, straining to breathe. "Not…Gilgamesh…"

As Lotus began to catch his breath, all of the comm screens came to life. Appearing on each of them was a man or woman. On the largest screen appeared President Evergreen, whom Lotus remembered meeting at the party on Muse.

"A pleasure to see you again, Mr. Lotus," the president said. "Welcome. I believe you already know Nicodemus, Gourd, and Mr. Wreath."

The three individuals identified nodded at Lotus, who said nothing.

EON

"The rest of those you see assembled before you and on the monitors make up the High Council of the League of Planets," President Evergreen continued. "You will forgive us for not being there personally, but for security reasons, only a select percentage of the High Council are allowed to physically meet at the same place at the same time. Members of the High Council, allow me to present to you Mr. Ian Lotus. Also known as Gilgamesh. Also known as Al Chronos."

Chaos ensued as most of the councilors began to talk at once.

"What is this, a joke?" asked one.

"This is insane," said another.

"You called an emergency session of the High Council for this?" asked a third.

The president called for order. "Quiet. Quiet, all of you."

Slowly, the room calmed down and a sense of order returned.

"Now," said the president, "I know how it must sound, but he *is* Gilgamesh...and Chronos."

All eyes turned to Lotus, who looked befuddled.

"What are all you people talking about?" Lotus asked.

"You can stop pretending," Gourd said. "We know who you are."

"Of course you do," Lotus agreed. "I met you only a day or two ago. I'm Ian Lotus."

"Yes, you are Ian Lotus," Gourd stated. "And many other men besides."

Lotus looked at him in utter disbelief. "You're insane." He looked around at the people assembled, both

EON

in person and digitally. "Anyone who would believe a word of this would have to be mad."

He turned to the newspaper owner. "Wreath, tell them how crazy this sounds."

"Sorry, but I'm on their side," Wreath said.

Lotus' eyes narrowed as a revelation came to him. "You brought the scorp-lion," he said to Wreath. Lotus glanced at Monica, who lowered her head in shame, and then back at Wreath. "You're the one who set me up."

Wreath laughed. "Well, I can't take all the credit. Sure, old Strike belonged to me, but it was Gourd here who came up with the test."

"You…you're as crazy as the rest of them," Lotus said.

"Please, Gil," Nicodemus said. "You're only wasting time by denying it. I should know; you and I fought side-by-side."

Lotus looked around in horror. "What's wrong with you people? Gilgamesh died sixty years ago, and Chronos twenty years before that. Even if they were still alive, they'd be old, old men."

"I agree," said one of the councilors on the monitors. "Mr. President, I don't know what game you're playing at, but I don't have time for this nonsense."

"You'll feel differently in a moment," President Evergreen said. "Play the recording."

There was silence for a second, and then a recording filled the room with the sound of coughing. Lotus was perplexed.

"I don't understand," stated another of the councilors. "What is this?"

"Just listen," Nicodemus said.

EON

A second recording began to play, also of someone coughing.

"Now, for an explanation," President Evergreen said. "The first tape you heard was a recording made sixty years ago during a raid on Gilgamesh's camp. Gas bombs were used in an effort to bring him in alive, but he escaped. The second recording was Mr. Lotus, a few minutes ago."

"I fail to see the point," the first councilor said. "What are you trying to prove?"

"Computer," Nicodemus said aloud. "Analysis."

"Analysis complete," said a computerized voice. "Ninety-eight point seven percent correlation."

The look of shock disappeared from Lotus' face, replaced by one of calm serenity. He relaxed, and a slight smile crept onto his lips.

"The computer analyzes voices for pitch, tone, resonance, and other factors," said Gourd.

"Anything over an eighty percent correlation is considered a match," Nicodemus added.

All eyes turned to Lotus, who grinned widely. "Let me save you the trouble of asking. It's true. I'm Gilgamesh."

Shock registered on the face of almost all those present.

"And Al Chronos?" asked Wreath.

"Yes," Lotus replied.

Monica inhaled sharply. "I knew it," she muttered under her breath.

All of a sudden the room was engulfed in noise as everyone spoke at once.

"Gilgamesh? Alive?"

"He's barely aged a day…"

EON

"This has to be some kind of trick…"

At the table, Wreath looked at Lotus in awe, mumbling, "It's really true."

"Don't start writing your headline just yet, Wreath," Nicodemus said. "None of this is printable. You are here only because we need your help to keep a lid on this thing, to keep it from becoming public knowledge."

Lotus turned to Nicodemus. "What's your connection to all this, Nick?"

"You said it yourself, Gil," Nicodemus replied. "I was always in the thick of things. I'm head of Interplanetary Intelligence, sometimes known as Galactic Intel."

Lotus nodded. "I should have known. This is so like you. I remember the ti—"

"Quiet! Quiet!" President Evergreen shouted, attempting to restore order.

"Mr. President, how long have you known about this?" asked one of the councilors on the monitors.

"About what?" the president queried in response.

"Him," the councilor said, pointing at Lotus. "You've been keeping hidden a man who hasn't aged a day in sixty years. Why?"

"I'll tell you why," answered one of his fellow councilors. "So he can get the secret for himself! So while the rest of us grow old and rot, he'll stay young and healthy."

Quite a few heads nodded in agreement with this statement.

"Alright, that's enough," said Evergreen testily. "Now you're all sounding as mad as Gilgamesh said we were a few minutes ago. I only recently found out about him, but we have a more pressing matter."

111

EON

"More pressing than immortality?" said one of the councilors rhetorically. "I don't think so. We want his secret."

"Yes, it's his secret we want," the president agreed, "but not what you're thinking, old fool."

"I believe I can enlighten you concerning that," Lotus began. "You see—"

"Guards!" shouted President Evergreen, cutting Lotus off. "Please escort Gilgamesh—"

"Actually, I prefer Ian," Lotus chimed in. "As far as I'm concerned, Gilgamesh died sixty years ago, and Chronos twenty years before that."

"Ian, then," the president acquiesced. "Guards, please escort our guests to their quarters. I have some matters to discuss with the council that will demand their full attention, and it involves Gil…I mean Ian, and I would prefer that he not overhear us."

Lotus and Monica rose as the guards came for them. As they were being escorted from the room, President Evergreen began speaking.

"What I am about to tell you is the greatest secret in the galaxy," the president began. "It is a secret that has been known by no more than five men at any one time in the past eighty years—"

The doors closed behind Lotus and Monica, cutting off the rest of the president's speech.

"Do you have any idea what he's talking about back there?" she asked.

A cocksure grin came across Ian's face. "As a matter of fact, I do."

"What? Tell me."

"Later."

EON

The guards led them into a room containing several jail cells. From what Lotus could tell, each cell had three walls and was bounded on the fourth side by an invisible force field. One of the guards punched some keys on a nearby keypad, causing the force field to shimmer slightly before disappearing.

"In with you," one of the guards said.

Monica and Lotus were roughly pushed inside. Lotus watched closely as the guard punched the keypad again, and the force field was reactivated. Lotus smiled to himself.

EON

Chapter 16

While Ian Lotus was busy being locked in a cell, President Evergreen was still behind locked doors, speaking to the High Council.

"There's not a single person alive who doesn't know about the Chronos Ring," Evergreen stated. "It is mankind's first and last line of defense against hostile alien races. Nothing can pass in or out of the Ring without a special passcode, and those passcodes are one of our most closely guarded secrets. However, three weeks ago, something unprecedented happened. Three Parsnaak warships passed through the Ring. Unharmed."

After a moment of stunned silence, pandemonium broke out, as — not for the first time that day — everyone shouted questions.

"What? How did this happen?"

"Why weren't we told sooner?"

Evergreen rolled his eyes in exhaustion. At this rate, they'd never get done.

****

Back in his cell, Lotus was testing the force field, using his hand. He applied pressure, but it didn't have any effect. Monica merely watched him, bemused.

"That's not going to work," she finally said.

"How do you know?" he asked.

"Because, everybody knows that you can't break through a force field. We'd have to get to the field generator controls, and they're way over there on that keypad. Just face it; we're stuck here until they let us out."

EON

"Maybe, maybe not," Lotus said, staring at the keypad and concentrating.

****

Back in the conference room, everyone was still talking at once.

"Nicodemus," said one of the councilors, "you're head of Intelligence. How was the Ring penetrated? Were our passcodes compromised?"

Nicodemus shook his head. "No, all of our codes were accounted for."

"What I want to know," said another member of the council, "is why our fleet didn't blow them to bits."

All eyes turned to Admiral Cohen, who — also on a monitor — appeared furious.

"What the hell are you talking about?" the admiral demanded. "We don't have a fleet. The Chronos Ring gave you all such a sense of security that you cut the military's manpower down to the bone. You don't give us money for men, weapons, or training. Yet in your hour of need, we're supposed to defend you? Let me ask, have any of you ever seen a Parsnaak warship? It's about as big as a small moon, with weapons pointing out of every square inch on its hull. Provided I could have scraped together enough men to field a fleet of ships, we would have been cut to pieces. All we could do was track them and monitor their activities. They could have blasted any one of a hundred habitable planets to bits, but they didn't."

There had been a bit of exaggeration in Admiral Cohen's rhetoric, but it was an effective speech nonetheless. Afterwards, silence reigned for a few moments.

"Wait a minute," asked one of the councilors. "If they didn't attack, then what did they do?"

EON

Chapter 17

Lotus was still staring at the keypad controlling the force field, so intensely focused that he almost forgot where he was.

Monica watched him, totally bewildered. "What are you—"

"Shhh!" Lotus hissed forcefully, not caring to have his concentration broken.

Monica immediately became silent. Looking across the room at the keypad, she watched as, slowly, first one number and then another was depressed by an invisible hand.

"Holy shit," she said under her breath.

As the last number was depressed, the force field shimmered and then disappeared. Lotus, breathing deeply, seemed to collapse in on himself for a moment, but quickly recovered.

"Come on," he said.

"What did you do?" Monica asked as they stepped out of their cell.

"I have a slight telekinetic ability. Nothing major. I can barely lift a pencil, and I have to concentrate like hell to do that."

Monica snapped her fingers, remembering something. "That's what happened to the Parsnaak in the alley on Muse. You pushed his hand — made him shoot his fellow soldier."

"Guess you're smarter than I thought. Let's get out of here." Swiftly, he retraced their steps out of the holding area.

"Not a bad idea," Monica noted, following him. "Those guys are going to be all over each other trying to see which of them gets the secret of immortality from you."

Lotus shook his head. "No. Unless I miss my guess, the secret of my longevity is — at best — only a secondary goal for them. There's an even bigger issue in play."

EON

Chapter 18

"You want to know what the Parsnaak did after entering human space?" Nicodemus asked, tackling the question that had been put before the council. "Their ships didn't divert one iota from their course. They had a specific destination in mind, and they went straight for it."

"What destination was that?" someone asked, plainly curious.

"The planet Muse," Nicodemus replied without hesitation.

"But why?" asked another.

"That's what we went there to find out," President Evergreen said. "As soon as we realized their destination, we used an upcoming exhibit as an excuse to make an appearance. By feigning a resurging interest in the arts, we hoped to uncover what the Parsnaak were after. Our best guess, at the moment, is that they came to kill Ian Lotus."

"Why do you say that?"

"Because over the past week," Nicodemus chimed in, "five men with a similar description have turned up dead."

"And do not overlook the fact that Ian Lotus — no matter what he calls himself — is also Al Chronos," Gourd added. "The man who developed the Ring. He is a man with a secret."

"He's a man with many secrets," the president said. "But right now, we're only interested in one."

"Yes," Wreath said with a sly, crafty smile. "Immortality."

EON

Nicodemus sighed in exasperation. "No, you idiot. He has an even bigger secret."

Nicodemus then began to explain.

EON

Chapter 19

Lotus stealthily peeked out of a doorway into a long corridor. Seeing no one, he crept out with Monica right behind him.

"I don't get it," she whispered. "If it's not the secret of immortality they want, then what is it?"

"They want the Ring's access code," Lotus answered.

They hid behind a bulkhead as someone approached. The person — a crewman — passed by without seeing them. After waiting a moment to make sure it was safe, they continued moving forward.

"What are you talking about?" Monica asked, picking up where she'd left off. "What access code?"

Lotus smiled smugly. "Contrary to popular belief, the Ring is not an actively controlled system. The government has spread the propaganda that the Ring is fully under its control, but the fact of the matter is that the Ring is completely autonomous."

"Explain that."

"If the Ring were actively controlled, there would be someone in charge who could make it fire at will, cease fire, or not fire at all. But there's no one who actually has the ability to do that — they'd need the access codes in order to have that kind of mastery of the Ring. As it is, no one has the access codes, so no one controls it."

EON

Chapter 20

Most of those in the conference room had trouble hiding their shock after Nicodemus explained their dilemma.

"Let me make sure I have this correct," said one of the councilors. "We do not control the Chronos Ring. No one does. We do not have the access code. No one does. If it breaks, we can't fix it. If it malfunctions, we can't fix it."

"Or make it fire on hostile enemies," Nicodemus added. "Or make it *not* fire on our own ships."

"Shit," murmured another of the councilors, who then turned to the president. "And you never told anyone? What kind of leader does that?"

Evergreen frowned in irritation. "As I previously said, there were always five people who knew, and that knowledge was only given to those who held certain offices. Those who learned of the situation did so by virtue of their position, not because of any favoritism."

"What about breaking the code?" asked someone else from one of the monitors. "Has anyone tried that?"

The question elicited an unexpected burst of laughter from Nicodemus.

"We've had teams of scientists working around the clock for the past eighty years trying to break the code," Admiral Cohen stated. "Of course, they have no idea of what they're really doing; they think they're working on a new encryption code for our military."

"Surely, in all that time, though, you must have had some breakthroughs," the first councilor asserted. "After all, Chronos was — *is* — only one man."

EON

Nicodemus, the admiral, and President Evergreen merely glanced at one another. After a moment, Gourd spoke up.

"Please, gentlemen, you must understand who you're dealing with here," the alien ambassador began. "We're talking about a man who has had hundreds, maybe even thousands, of years to perfect every skill, every talent, every ability at his disposal. We have our brightest scientists — human and otherwise — working on deciphering the necessary algorithms to obtain the access code. However, whereas the most senior among our scientists may have decades of experience in this field, the man who currently calls himself Ian Lotus is likely to have centuries."

At that moment, a young guard entered the room. He headed straight for Nicodemus, bending over and whispering in the older man's ear.

"Then why are we waiting?" another councilor asked. "Let's get him back in here."

"That might be a little harder than it sounds," Nicodemus announced. "He's escaped."

EON

Chapter 21

Monica and Lotus crept quietly down a hallway, looking for an exit.

"You still haven't told me why you kept the access code a secret," she said.

Lotus seemed to ponder for a moment before he responded. "When I first invented the Ring, humanity was in trouble. The Parsnaak were kicking our asses from one side of the galaxy to the other, and the Corsians were playing both ends against the middle. Man didn't have any allies back then — none that were willing to die beside him, anyway. Our initial hope back then was just to be able to hold our own. But after the Ring came online, things changed. We had an invincible weapon, and there were certain people who felt we should use it. They wanted to continually expand the Ring outward, conquering as we went. That would have made us as bad as the Parsnaak, but when I said so, I was shouted down. Overruled."

"Outvoted."

"Yes. Out*voted*, but not out*smarted*. That's when I introduced the access code into the Ring. Without it, the Ring stays in its current position and in a passive mode. It only fires on ships not having a passcode."

"And then you disappeared."

"As Al Chronos, yes."

At that moment, they passed a porthole. Lotus peered out.

"Oh, jeez," he muttered.

"What is it?"

EON

When he didn't immediately answer, Monica pushed him aside to get a look herself. She saw that they were out among the stars.

"We're not on New Onyx anymore," Lotus said wearily. "We're somewhere in space."

He stood there silently, reflecting on exactly what that meant. The sound of klaxons going off a moment later, however, quickly brought Lotus back to himself.

"I think they know we're gone," he said. "We have to hurry."

He ran down the hallway, with Monica in tow.

"Where are we going?" she asked while practically being dragged along.

"The landing bay," he said, still running.

They had been lucky enough to avoid detection thus far, Lotus realized, but luck had a tendency to run out. That seemed to be the case when, as they rounded a corner, Lotus and Monica ran into two guards. Lotus immediately jumped up and kicked one in the face. The man staggered back into the wall, and then slumped, unconscious, to the floor.

As he came back down, Lotus immediately dropped down low and swept the legs out from under the second guard, who landed flat on his back and didn't move. The second guard's gun clattered to the floor next to Monica, who picked it up.

Lotus bent over the second guard and began to remove his uniform.

"Help me get his clothes off," Lotus said. "It'll be a tight fit, but maybe it can fool someone long enough for us to get a shuttle and get off this boat."

EON

Monica didn't answer, prompting Lotus to glance behind him. To his surprise, Monica aimed the guard's gun at him. She fired, and everything went black.

EON

Chapter 22

Lotus awoke to find himself strapped into a large metal chair, his arms and legs cuffed. Electrodes were connected all over his body. He was still dressed in the clothes he had been wearing, which — thankfully — implied that they had probably only checked him for weapons. (He also wasn't dead, which meant that the gun he'd been shot with had obviously been set on "stun.")

In the room with him were Nicodemus, Monica, Gourd, and Wreath. This room, like the conference room he'd been in before, had a large number of monitors through which members of the High Council were watching.

"He is awake," Gourd said.

"I'm sorry this can't be more pleasant for you, Ian," the president began, "but we are pressed for time, and we need answers yesterday."

"That's okay, Mr. President," Lotus said. "And to show there are no hard feelings, I'm going to make it a point to give you the same kind of hospitality you've shown me the next time we meet."

Evergreen laughed nervously. "I look forward to it. But for now, let's proceed."

Nicodemus turned to Lotus. "What is your name?"

Lotus merely stared at him.

"What is your name?" Nicodemus repeated.

Lotus remained silent.

"Is your name Ian Lotus?" Nicodemus asked.

"No, it's Robin Hood," Lotus answered.

An electric shock suddenly hit Lotus, making him arch his back and yell in pain.

EON

Monica looked away.

Gourd smiled at Lotus' discomfort. "You have just made the acquaintance of a crude but effective lie detector. Each time you lie, you will receive a shock, but with each lie the amount of voltage grows. Now tell us again, are you Ian Lotus?"

"No, I'm the Pied Piper," Lotus said, then screamed as he was shocked again.

"Please, Ian," Monica implored, looking misty-eyed. "Just tell them. Tell them what they want to know."

Lotus glared at her. "Thanks for the advice, *friend*. Never let it be said that you ran out on me."

Monica lowered her head a bit shamefully.

"I'd appreciate it if you'd go a little easier on my granddaughter, Ian," Nicodemus said.

Lotus stared at him in disbelief, then glanced at Monica.

"Granddaughter?" Lotus said, almost as if he didn't know what the word meant.

"Yes. Lovely, isn't she?" Nicodemus said with pride. "And an excellent operative."

Lotus' brow crinkled as his mind flitted back in time, rooting out old facts.

"You had a daughter. Nica," he said to Nicodemus. "Monica's *her* daughter."

Nicodemus smiled. "She'll be pleased that you remember her. It would also be nice if I could tell her that her hero Gilgamesh just saved humanity…again."

Ian was silent for a moment, obviously contemplating something. Finally, he let out a deep breath. "My name is Ian Lotus."

"And Gilgamesh?" Gourd asked.

EON

"And Gilgamesh," Lotus confirmed. "And Al Chronos."

The room was suddenly filled with a deafening level of commotion as numerous people — most of whom were trying to address Lotus — began speaking simultaneously.

"One at a time," Nicodemus insisted, raising his hands for order. "One person at a time."

It took a few minutes, but slowly, a sense of calm asserted itself and spread across the room.

One of the councilors took advantage of the ensuing silence to ask a question of Lotus. "How have you lived so long?"

Lotus shrugged. "I don't know."

"Do you have any theory?" asked another.

Lotus didn't immediately respond, as he seemingly pondered the question.

"I was born in the latter half of the twentieth century," he finally said, "in a country known as the United States. I was raised by my mother. My father disappeared shortly after my third birthday; I have no recollection of him.

"As a teenager, I signed up for military service, mostly because I didn't know what else to do with myself. I never expected to fight, but ended up battling for my life in some hellhole on the other side of the planet. The guys we were fighting released a nerve gas, some kind of toxin. The lucky ones died right away, although some lingered on for days. You could hear them, day and night, screaming in pain. I was one of them, but for some reason I recovered and survived. I was the only one who did.

EON

"The doctors said there were some 'genetic anomalies' in my gene structure, but they didn't know if it was an adaptive measure my body took as a result of the toxin, or a pre-existing condition that allowed me to survive it. I didn't know and I didn't care. All I knew was that I'd lost my entire unit – almost everybody I cared about. It took me years to recover emotionally, but when I did, I discovered that I hadn't aged. My assumption, then, is that the toxin somehow mutated my body and slowed the aging process."

Silence reigned while those assembled took a few moments to digest what they'd heard. The fact that the lie detector hadn't shocked Lotus meant that he was telling the truth (or, at least the truth as he believed it).

"I'm curious about something," Wreath said. "Why didn't you ever change your appearance? The streak in your hair, your face…or just gotten rid of that pendant?"

"I was already having to change my name every few years," Lotus replied. "I was afraid that if I started changing my appearance, too, I'd eventually forget who I was. As for the streak, my mother told me that she dropped me when I was a toddler and I injured my head. There was no permanent damage, except the hair grew back white. It's the only thing I have left to remind me of her. As for the pendant, she told me that it was an heirloom from my father's side of the family. I wear it as a testament to him."

Admiral Cohen harrumphed gruffly. "I'm touched by all of this family sentiment, but I think we need to get down to business. We currently have three Parsnaak warships within the Ring. Our long-range sensors detect an entire fleet moving towards us. It will reach the

EON

outermost boundary of the Ring in two days. We have no fleet, no manning, and if they have found a way to circumvent the Ring — which it seems they have — we have no defenses. In short, we need the access code so that we may, at the very least, actively control the Ring and have it fire on any Parsnaak vessel that enters."

"Beta two nine gamma vertigo," Lotus said without hesitation.

Gourd began typing on a nearby console. "Code entered. Two minutes to upload."

A silent, lingering tension slowly filled the room as those present waited to see whether the alleged access code would work.

"I have a question for you," Lotus said, speaking to Gourd. "This situation concerns humanity, so why is a Corsian involved?"

"Because he is an ambassador from his world," President Evergreen interjected, "and represents his people on the High Council. Also, a significant number of aliens, Corsian and otherwise, currently live in human-occupied space. Many of them do so just for the protection offered by the Chronos Ring. It is, therefore, in their best interest to assist us."

"Also," Gourd added. "My entire clave — what you would call family — currently resides inside the Ring. By helping you, I protect them."

The Corsian turned back to his keyboard. "Upload is complete, and the code is…not accepted."

"What?" Lotus uttered in surprise as all eyes swiveled towards him.

A small triangular object near Gourd's keyboard projected a hologram into the air, consisting of unusual letters and symbols that scrolled across from left to right.

EON

Gourd stared at the symbols and released a distressful groan. "As I said, the code is not being accepted."

"Let me see that," Lotus said, nodded towards the holographic symbols.

Nicodemus took the triangular object projecting the hologram and brought it over to Lotus, who stared at the symbols intently.

"Oh shit," Lotus said after a moment.

"What is it?" asked Wreath. "What's happening?"

"Someone's blocking our code," Lotus responded.

The president frowned. "Who? How?"

Lotus shook his head in incomprehension. "I don't know, but they are inputting a corruption code at the Ring's primary site."

He looked around at the others who were present.

"Please," Lotus said, "you have to let me go. I can fix this, but only at the primary site."

No one said anything, and Lotus could sense their hesitation at the thought of letting him go.

"Why can't you simply tell our people and have them fix it?" one of the councilors finally asked.

"Because I understand the Chronos Ring," Lotus answered indignantly. "I built the damn thing. I can analyze, diagnose, and repair damage ten times faster than someone who's unfamiliar with it. You know we don't have much time. You have to let me go."

"Considering what we know about this man," said another member of the council, "and the secrets he carries, I'm wary of letting him out of our sight."

"I feel the same," piped in another. "If we should lose him, just think of what we'd have given up."

EON

"Yeah, the secret of immortality," Lotus said snarkily. "Well, it's not going to do you much good when you're slaving in a Parsnaak mine pit. Think about doing that for the next thousand years and see how well you sleep tonight. Frankly speaking, we don't have time for this. You need to let me go *now*."

Lotus' demand seemed to trigger an avalanche of discussion, as the pros and cons of what he'd just said were weighed by those present. Much to his surprise, several members of the High Council were in favor of letting him go — a fact that didn't sit well with Gourd.

"Mr. President," the Corsian said. "I propose that we discuss the issue of whether to release Ian Lotus behind closed doors. That way, there will be little outside influence" — he looked directly at Lotus — "on anyone's decision."

"Very well," the president said, agreeing. "Everyone physically present meet in the conference room in five minutes."

Everyone began filing out of the room.

"What about him?" Gourd said, indicating Lotus, who was still strapped in place.

"I'll keep an eye on him," Monica said. Her grandfather gave her an inquiring look, but she ushered him out along with everyone else. "Go. I'll be fine."

A moment later, only she and Lotus were left in the room. She walked back towards Lotus with a look on her face that seemed to indicate that she wanted to talk.

"Why are you still here?" he practically demanded before she could say a word. "You'd better hurry up and join the others, or you'll miss out on new and exciting ways to stab people in the back."

"I was just doing my job," she said.

EON

"Which consisted of setting me up the entire time we were together. You're how they tracked me down on New Onyx. You're how those soldiers found me in that bar back on Muse."

"Yes. I've been keeping them updated on our movements."

"And that cyborg that you said hired you. You made it all up. That's why he didn't know what the hell I was talking about."

Monica nodded. "I needed you to stay put until the soldiers showed up. You were convinced someone had hired me, so I just fed into that belief."

Lotus shook his head at his own gullibility. "I must have been the easiest assignment you ever had."

"Actually, you were a tough guy to get close to," she admitted. "Even though I had the inside track."

"Inside track?" he repeated.

"My grandfather told me that you had a soft spot for women in distress."

"Which you then exploited by pretending to constantly be afraid and in need of protection. I'm an idiot."

Monica reached out and took his head in her hands. He initially flinched, unsure of what she was up to, and then she bent down and gave him a kiss.

"I never wanted to hurt you," she said after drawing back a moment later.

"No, just use me," Lotus clarified.

Monica looked at him as though he had punched her in the gut. Fighting to hold back tears, she walked toward the exit. She turned back to him just before she left the room.

EON

"I didn't like what I did, but I was asked to do a tough job," she said. "Gilgamesh allowed himself to be branded a murderer and a terrorist in order to shine a light on an injustice. That showed me that sometimes the world is going to hate you for the things you do, even if what you're doing is right. I thought you of all people would understand that."

She slammed the door behind her as she left.

EON

Chapter 23

The discussion regarding Lotus was in full swing when Monica entered the conference room. If anyone wondered why she wasn't with Lotus at the moment, they didn't voice their concerns.

"I still say we cannot trust him," Gourd was stressing. "We have no idea of where his true allegiance lies."

"Besides which," said a member of the High Council, "the man's much more formidable than he appears at first glance. Especially when you consider this new revelation about his telekinesis."

"He's only slightly telekinetic," Nicodemus clarified.

"Correction," said another of the councilors. "He only *told* you he's slightly telekinetic. For all we know, he could be a full-blown psychic."

"I'm afraid I have to agree," said President Evergreen. "Ian Lotus is simply too random a variable to risk even the possibility of him escaping. Yet, we can't just stand idly by and allow a hostile alien race annihilate us."

"Gentlemen," Gourd said. "I believe I may have a viable solution…"

****

Back in the other room, Lotus' ears were burning; it was pretty clear that he was the topic of the High Council's conversation at the moment. For the umpteenth time, he labored against the restraints holding him in place, but to no avail. They seemed to have been

EON

designed almost with him in mind. (And maybe they had been, considering what his captors knew about him.) Still, if he couldn't escape by brute force, maybe there was something else he could try.

He was still lost in thought, trying to formulate a plan of escape, when a vertical line of light appeared in the room.

"Oh fuck," Lotus said to himself as, unsurprisingly, the gargantuan form of Obsidian began to exit the shaft of light. Next to the colossus was a shimmering outline that was humanoid in appearance.

"Kill him, Obsidian," said a queer voice — the same voice Lotus had heard on Muse and New Onyx. "Kill the pretender."

In acknowledgment of this order, Obsidian began walking towards Lotus just as the door opened up and Monica came in. Obsidian ignored her and continued towards his target.

On his part, Lotus lunged against the straps and cuffs holding him down. The metal of the chair creaked and groaned but wouldn't give in; it was old, but clearly built to last. He wasn't going anywhere — a fact that didn't bode well considering the fact that the monstrously large Obsidian now loomed over him in a clearly menacing fashion.

Monica dashed to the keyboard Gourd had been seated at and began rapidly hitting the keys just as Obsidian, now standing over Lotus, locked his fingers together and raised his hands above his head for a killing blow.

Unexpectedly, the restraints on his arms and legs opened, releasing Lotus just as Obsidian smashed down. Almost too fast to be believed, Lotus dove between

EON

Obsidian's legs just as the giant's blow came down and crushed the metal chair.

Lotus tried to rise, but was caught as Obsidian swiftly turned around and grabbed him in a bear hug. Lotus' face immediately contorted with pain as his assailant squeezed.

Behind Obsidian, Monica fired her lasergun into the giant's back. It had no effect.

"Shoot…" Lotus muttered, grimacing against the pain. "Shoot…"

"It doesn't work against him!" Monica yelled in a flustered tone.

"Floor…" Lotus managed to get out. "Shoot…floor…"

Now understanding, Monica fired a shot at the floor beneath Obsidian's feet. It vanished in a flash, and both Lotus and his assailant dropped like stones.

They fell through to the floor beneath them, with Lotus having the good fortune to land on top. Obsidian, slightly stunned by the fall, loosened his grip and Lotus slipped away. Monica, still in the room above them, immediately fired at the floor beneath Obsidian once Lotus was clear, sending the giant crashing down yet again. She then jumped down and joined Lotus.

"Come on," she said, grabbing his hand and pulling him towards a nearby door.

"Where are we going?" he asked as they stepped out into a hallway.

Still holding his hand, Monica led him through the ship at breakneck speed. "You got your wish. The council agreed to let you go, but on one condition."

"Which is?"

"That we go with you."

EON

Lotus frowned. "*We?* Who's *we?*"

At that moment, they rounded a corner and found themselves in the landing bay. Not far away, standing next to a sleek new spaceship, were Gourd and Nicodemus.

"We means the three of us," Monica said. "Your crew."

"Great," Lotus said, not caring that he sounded particularly sarcastic.

He and Monica ran towards the ship. As they drew closer, Lotus began giving orders.

"Nick, Gourd," he said, getting their attention. "Get on board now. We leave immediately."

Lotus sprinted up the open entry ramp and into the ship without waiting to see whether anyone else would follow. A few moments later, the other three joined him, with Gourd mindfully closing the door behind them.

"Strap in," Lotus ordered roughly. "We're taking off."

He hopped into the pilot's seat and initiated the takeoff procedure; through the ship's observation window, the landing bay doors could be seen as they began to open.

"Taking off?" Nicodemus said quizzically. "We haven't even loaded all the supplies yet."

"Listen," Lotus said forcefully. "This little expedition has been authorized because of *my* suggestion and proceeds under *my* direction, and I say we leave right now, supplies or not."

Gourd seemed dismissive of Lotus' statement, saying, "Our mission is urgent, but I think it unwise to

EON

leave without being fully prepared. Is there a reason for your haste?

"Yeah," Lotus said. "*That.*"

Pointing out the observation window, he indicated a spot in the landing bay where Obsidian's arm had just driven up through the floor.

"Well, I'm glad that's our only emergency," Monica said. "I thought you were going to say it was *that.*"

She pointed towards the open landing bay doors, where a huge Parsnaak warship could be seen heading towards them. Lotus hit a few buttons, and the scene on the observation window — which could also serve as a viewscreen of areas outside the craft — changed. It now showed a close-up view of the approaching craft, which had its guns pointed in their direction. As if on cue, the Parsnaak vessel began to shoot.

The spaceship was pounded by the firepower of the Parsnaak vessel, with alarms suddenly going off from stem to stern. Aboard their smaller craft, Lotus and his companions strapped themselves in and prepared to take off.

Ignoring protocol and procedure, Lotus turned their standard engines up to maximum and immediately sent their craft rocketing out through the bay doors, roaring past Obsidian, who was just pulling himself up through the floor.

They had barely cleared the ship before Lotus shouted, "Coordinates are loaded! Prepare for hyperdrive!"

Behind them, the spacecraft they just left exploded, the shock wave rocking them violently. The Parsnaak ship began turning its guns in their direction.

EON

Just as they fired, Lotus and his companions zoomed into hyperspace.

EON

Chapter 24

Once in hyperspace, Lotus let out a long, ragged breath as the ship stopped its violent motion and became stable. That one had been too close.

"Is anyone injured?" Gourd asked.

"No, I think we're all fine," Nicodemus answered, then turned to Lotus. "I take it we're heading to the Ring's primary site."

"That's our final destination," Lotus said.

"And what happens when we get there?" Nicodemus asked.

"I try to find out what's blocking the access code," Lotus replied.

Monica, who had been listening, asked, "What exactly is this primary site?"

"Well, the Chronos Ring is actually made up of huge spheres," Nicodemus explained. "The primary site is the sphere that houses the main computer program that keeps the Ring going. It's also located at the place where Al Chronos invented the Ring technology."

"'Invented' is actually a bit of a misnomer," Lotus said. "What actually happened was that, for a brief moment, some kind of hole in space opened up and a stream of data rushed out. It was really advanced stuff; a scientist could have made a career out of it. I was able to decipher a portion of it, and that portion is what became the Chronos Ring."

"They must have been extremely sophisticated," Gourd opined, "the race that sent the data stream. Just the small portion you were able to intercept and decode has provided your race with benefits that will last for over

EON

a thousand years. Perhaps we can expect another such event."

"Too bad you won't get the opportunity," said a new voice.

Looking in the direction of the speaker, Lotus saw Wreath brandishing a lasergun. He stood near a door that led to the other compartments of the ship, and had obviously stowed away prior to their hasty escape from the Parsnaak attack.

Nicodemus stared at the media mogul in shock and fury. "Wreath, what the hell are you doing here? This isn't some party you can crash and get a story out of."

"Shut up, you old windbag," Wreath said in response. "Now, hands up — all of you."

Everyone raised their hands. Wreath stalked over and, motioning Lotus away, began to manipulate the ship's controls.

"What do you think you're doing?" Nicodemus asked.

Wreath smiled wickedly. "Just taking a little detour. I'm eager to have a private talk with our friend here."

"We can't take a detour," Monica began insistently. "There's a Parsnaak fleet—"

"I know all about the fleet," Wreath stated, cutting her off, "and I don't give a damn. The only thing I care about is his secret — and I don't mean any damned access code."

"You mean his longevity?" Nicodemus concluded. "You heard him before; he doesn't know how it happened."

EON

"Bullshit," Wreath spat out. "Somehow he fooled the lie detector, but he knows; he just hasn't told. But he will."

There was silence for a moment, and then Monica asked, "Why are you doing this?"

Wreath answered without hesitation. "Because I'm sick. Very, *very* sick. Now it's not something really visible on the outside — at least not yet — but the docs only give me a year to live. So, I'm here to get his secret."

"But what good will it do you if we're all conquered by the Parsnaak?" Monica asked.

Wreath snorted derisively. "You think I'm not prepared? I'm one of the richest men in the galaxy. I've got my own secret mansion — fully automated — hidden beneath the surface of a distant planet with enough supplies stocked to feed a city for a thousand years. No, little lady, I am fully prepared. I'll still be alive and kicking long after everyone's forgotten what a Parsnaak ever was. All I need now is his secret."

He turned to Lotus. "Now, you tell me the truth, or I start killing folks. Beginning with her." Wreath pointed his weapon at Monica.

"There's no need for that," Lotus said. "I'll tell you."

His companions now looked at Lotus in surprise.

"But I thought you said—" Monica began.

"Never mind what I said," Lotus blurted out, not giving her a chance to finish. "If it'll save your life, then it's worth it."

Lotus looked at Wreath. "You're right — I did fool the lie detector. The true secret of my long life is this pendant around my neck. It's an ancient relic from a lost civilization on a forgotten world. However, as long as I wear it, I don't age. Here, I'll show you."

All eyes had shifted to the relic Lotus wore as he spoke. He now reached up with both hands to remove it.

"Not so fast," Wreath suddenly said. "I'll take it off."

Keeping his weapon trained on Lotus, Wreath stepped forward and reached for the necklace. Grabbing the chain holding the pendant, he tightened his grip, clearly preparing to forcefully yank it off Lotus' neck. However, before he could do so, he was hit with a powerful surge of electricity. Wreath screamed in pain, and his hair stood on end as high voltage shot through his body. Finally, he let go and collapsed with serious burns all over his body.

Lotus nonchalantly bent down and took Wreath's gun, and then reset the ship's final coordinates.

Still surprised by what had happened, Nicodemus asked, "What did you do to him?"

"Me?" Lotus said innocently. "Nothing. It was the pendant. It shocks anyone who tries to take it off."

"Even you?" asked Gourd.

Lotus shook his head. "No, because I don't try to take it off. As a matter of fact, it won't come off."

"Now you're being silly," Monica chimed in.

"No, I'm not," Lotus replied.

"Can't you break it?" Nicodemus asked.

"No," Lotus said, "and at first I was scared shitless, so I had a metallurgist look at it. He said it wasn't metal. Since then, I've just learned to accept it, and it's even come in handy on a few occasions, like just now."

EON

Lotus' words brought Wreath to mind, and Monica glanced at the media mogul. He appeared to be semi-conscious, moaning in obvious pain.

"What should we do with him?" she asked.

"Nothing for now," Lotus said, "except maybe roll him into a corner or put him in back so he doesn't get in the way."

Without warning, the ship suddenly dropped out of hyperspace.

"We would appear to have arrived," Gourd said, stating the obvious.

The observation window showed a large, orange-red planet near them.

"I don't understand," Monica said to Lotus. "I thought you said we were going to the Ring."

"No," he corrected, "I said the Ring was our *final* destination."

"Then where are we?" Gourd asked.

"System A-V-Three-Six-G," Lotus said. "There are no inhabitable worlds in it, so nobody's bothered to give it a more palatable name."

"I take it the same goes for the planet on the viewscreen," Nicodemus said.

"Yeah, it's just Planet VII of this system," Lotus replied.

"So why are we here?" Monica asked.

Lotus looked at each of those present in turn and then sighed. "I'm afraid I haven't been completely honest with you."

"I'm shocked," Monica said, her voice heavy with sarcasm. "So what else is new?"

Lotus ignored her. "Look, there are two ways to control the Ring. One is with the access code, and can be done remotely. The other is through direct entry on the command console at the primary site."

"Well, we already know the first option isn't working," Nicodemus said.

"Exactly," Lotus agreed with a nod, "which is why we have to go to the Ring itself."

"So that begs the question," Gourd said. "Why are we *here*?" He tilted his head towards the planet showing through the observation window.

"We can't just show up at the Ring's primary site, waltz in, and do whatever we like," Lotus said. "There are safeguards against that. In short, we need a key."

"Let me guess," Nicodemus said. "There's only one key, and you have it."

Lotus smiled. "Good guess. But to be more precise, there's only one key, but in three pieces — one of which is on the planet below."

"And the other two components of the key?" Gourd asked.

Lotus drummed his fingers for a moment, obviously thinking, then seemed to come to a decision of sorts. "I already have the other parts of the key."

"Wait a minute," Monica said, snapping her fingers. "Those two boxes you retrieved on Muse and New Onyx. They weren't just for trying to scan the Ring. They held pieces of the key."

"Very good," Lotus said with a smile.

Nicodemus looked at his granddaughter. "But you said he destroyed the components of the first box, and everything in the second got blasted to bits when the Parsnaak attacked you on New Onyx."

"He must have slipped something into his pocket when I wasn't watching the first time," Monica said, giving Lotus an evil glare. "With the second box, he already had it open when I woke up."

"Look, it doesn't matter how I got the first two parts of the key," Lotus insisted. "Our issue now is getting the last piece."

"Then let us proceed," Gourd said.

"We will," stated Lotus, "but first, there are some things you three need to know."

"Such as?" Monica inquired.

"For starters," Lotus said, "that planet you see outside — in fact, this entire system — doesn't exist."

Nicodemus frowned in confusion. "What do you mean they don't exist?"

"What I mean," answered Lotus, "is that you won't find them listed in any database, registry, index, directory, or catalog. Thus, for practically all intents and purposes, they aren't there."

"How's that possible?" asked a truly perplexed Monica.

"Do you not understand?" Gourd asked. "Ian Lotus has purged every trace of them from all extant records — a remarkable feat."

"All to protect the location of one component of a key?" Monica wondered aloud.

"There's more than just a piece of a key here," Lotus stated. "This planet is one of the manufacturing sites for the spheres that make up the Ring."

The other three suddenly stared at Lotus in bug-eyed surprise.

"What?" he continued. "You thought those spheres just dropped out of the ether? No — they get made on planets like this, and if they start to glitch or malfunction, they automatically return for repair."

EON

As if to give proof to Lotus' words, a gargantuan sphere — obviously part of the Ring — suddenly appeared in space above the planet. It had obviously dropped out of hyperspace, and immediately began descending towards the world below.

"Incredible..." Monica murmured, watching the scene through the viewscreen. She then looked towards Lotus. "So, who runs all this?"

"Nobody," Lotus answered. "The process is fully automated — has been for decades now."

"So what are we waiting for?" Nicodemus said. "Let's get down there, get the missing part of the key, and go fix the Ring."

"A few ground rules first," Lotus said. "There's a landing platform at the manufacturing site. We'll set down there, and then I'll go get the third piece of the key. The rest of you will stay aboard this craft."

"That strikes me as foolish," Gourd stated, "on our part. You have already shown yourself to be incredibly capable and resourceful. Even more, you plan ahead. Who is to say that you do not have another vessel secreted away planetside that you will use to escape and vanish once again after leaving us here?"

"That's an interesting point," Lotus said. "Unfortunately, I don't have time to prove to you that I have no plans to desert you. The truth of the matter is that it's dangerous down there."

"Dangerous?" Gourd reported. "In what sense? You said the planet was uninhabited."

"I should clarify," Lotus said. "The air is unbreathable — toxic, in fact — so life as we know it doesn't exist down there, but there's...something."

EON

Monica crossed her arms and gave Lotus a firm stare. "You're going to have to do better than that, Ian."

"Look, I can't really describe it, okay?" Lotus said. "It's some kind of life-form that we never encountered elsewhere and were never quite able to classify. It doesn't seem to have a problem with machines, but organic life…well, it seems to have issues with us."

"Be that as it may," Gourd said, "it would be unwise to leave you unescorted, even on a planet such as you described."

"Fine," Lotus said irritably. "Pick who you want to die. Or draw straws. Whatever. I don't care."

"There's no need for a decision by lots," said the alien ambassador. "I have no plans on letting you out of my sight. I will accompany you, regardless of what danger may be lurking about."

Lotus shrugged. "It's your funeral. Let me know how you'd like your headstone to read."

EON

Chapter 25

"What's taking them so long?" Monica asked, anxiously staring at the viewscreen. "I'm starting to get a bad feeling."

"It's barely been an hour," Nicodemus noted. "Be patient."

Monica nodded, trying to mimic her grandfather's calm. Plus, he was right: objectively, not a great deal of time had gone by. Still, she couldn't shake the feeling that something was wrong.

They had docked on the unnamed planet without incident, touching down on a landing platform, as had previously been suggested. Donning atmospheric suits, Lotus and Gourd had then left their craft, with the former saying that they would be back in about an hour. They had remained in voice communication with the ship for about a hundred yards, at which point they had turned a corner and the transmission had gone silent. (Apparently something in the atmosphere made communications difficult without a direct line of sight.) Since then, there had been nothing but apprehensive waiting, which grew more intense with each passing minute.

Suddenly, Monica caught sight of Lotus rounding a corner. At the same time, the comm crackled, coming to life and broadcasting his static-filled voice.

"—en…hatch…" his voice said.

"Something's wrong," she said, noting that Lotus' image on the viewscreen seemed to be moving in an odd manner, almost as though he was wobbling. She enhanced the picture, magnifying the scene, and then realized what the issue was: Lotus was carrying one of the

EON

metal boxes she had seen before with one hand. With the other, he balanced Gourd on his shoulder as he raced back towards their ship.

"Open the fucking hatch!" Lotus screamed. This time, the words came through loud and clear. "Now!"

"Shit!" yelled Nicodemus, noting that something like a boulder with legs was lumbering behind Lotus — and gaining.

Monica, sitting at the controls, didn't comment. Instead, she hit the switch for the exterior hatch and turned on the engines. She had the ship float up vertically about a foot from the platform, and then raised the landing gear.

"Come on," she said, watching Lotus run and hearing his exhausted breathing coming through the comm relay. "Hurry…"

A second later, he passed from view, in one of the blind spots of the exterior cameras.

"Go!" Lotus' voice suddenly boomed.

Monica, hand already on the controls, sent them zooming away almost before the word was out of Lotus' mouth. On the viewscreen, she saw the rock-thing standing on the platform, silently watching their hasty retreat.

****

"It was pretty much fine up until the point where I retrieved the box," Lotus said later. "It was in a hidden panel in a repair station within an underground section of the manufacturing facility."

"So what happened?" Monica asked.

EON

"We were still below the surface when one of the underground walls just seemed to come alive," he replied. "It batted Gourd aside like a gnat. It came after me, but I made some evasive maneuvers and was able to scoop up Gourd. Then I hightailed it back."

Although he had been knocked unconscious, Gourd only suffered superficial injuries. It was more fortunate for him that his atmospheric suit hadn't suffered any catastrophic damage.

"My thanks to you for saving my life," said the Corsian ambassador, now awake. "However, you are partly at fault for my injuries."

"How's that?" Lotus asked.

Gourd stared at him sternly. "You placed the third piece of the key on an inhospitable planet with an unbreathable atmosphere where it was guarded by monsters."

"So?" Lotus said.

"So you made it damn near impossible to retrieve," Nicodemus said.

"That was the point!" Lotus blurted out, as if it were a universal truth.

"Excuse me," Monica interjected, "but can we debate the merits of Ian's hiding place *after* we fix the Chronos Ring and save the human race?"

"Ah, sure," Lotus said, somewhat sheepishly, then began inputting new coordinates for the hyperdrive.

EON

Chapter 26

"It appears that we have arrived," Gourd announced as the ship dropped out of hyperspace.

Through the viewscreen, Lotus and the others saw that they had reached the Chronos Ring.

"Which sphere is the primary site?" asked Monica.

Gourd pointed to a sphere noticeably larger than all the others. "I would say that one."

Lotus nodded. "Good guess."

He maneuvered the ship closer. As the primary site came more into view, they all saw a sliver of light – coming from a hole in space – striking the surface of the sphere directly.

"What is that?" Monica asked.

"Our problem," said her grandfather.

Lotus started tapping the keys on a nearby console.

"He's right," said Lotus. "It's a data stream, and it's corrupting the protocols established in the Chronos Ring. I'm going to try to—"

He stopped as the pendant around his neck suddenly began to rise as if by magic. The chain holding it snapped as the pendant floated out into the middle of the room. Suddenly, it began to spin.

"Any idea what's happening?" asked Nicodemus.

"None whatsoever," Lotus said. "At a guess, I'd say it's responding to the data stream."

"Or the data stream source," Gourd countered.

Lotus contemplated this and was about to comment when the comm unit roared to life. At the same time, the image on the viewscreen suddenly changed. On

EON

it was a man in an unfamiliar uniform of some sort, speaking a strange language.

"What's he saying?" asked Monica.

"Make love, not war," Lotus replied.

Monica's eyebrows lifted in surprise. "Really?"

"How the hell should I know?" Lotus said, throwing his hands up in exasperation.

Without warning, the uniformed man disappeared from the screen. At that exact moment, a vertical line of light appeared in the middle of the ship.

"Oh no," Monica muttered, while Lotus — now recognizing the slit of light as some kind of dimensional rift (and a telltale sign of Obsidian's imminent appearance) — yelled for everyone to arm themselves.

Instead of Obsidian, however, the uniformed man stepped through, causing Monica and Lotus to both let out sighs of relief. All of them now saw that the man was a soldier of some sort, with a weapon at his hip. He seemed unconcerned by the fact that he was alone among strangers. He stepped up and grabbed the spinning pendant, then looked around at each of the four people present.

"Where did you get this?" the soldier asked no one in particular.

"You speak our language," Nicodemus noted.

The newcomer ignored him. Instead, he traced the outline of a sunburst design on the pendant.

"This bears the sigil of the Eonian Royal House," the soldier said, still staring at the relic. "It is not allowed in common hands."

"Are you saying we shall be punished for using it?" asked Gourd.

EON

The soldier laughed. "Punished? It is death just to have it!"

Lotus and his companions shared nervous glances.

"I ask you again," the soldier continued, "where did you get this?"

"It's mine," Lotus admitted. "It belonged to my father."

"Ha!" the soldier laughed. "This could not—"

His voice came to a halt as he took a moment to simply stare at Lotus. He then pressed a button on the waist of his uniform.

"This is a matter for my superiors," he stated. "I have sent for an escort."

"An escort?" repeated Nicodemus. "For what? Where are we going?"

"I'm sorry," Lotus interjected before the soldier could answer, "but we don't have time to wait for your escort to arrive. We've got less than forty-eight hours to get what I assume is your corrupted data out of our system."

"There's no need to wait," the soldier said. "They are here."

On the viewscreen, as if out of nowhere, Lotus saw gigantic ships appearing around their craft.

"Now what?" Monica asked their visitor.

"Now you go before Eon," the soldier replied.

EON

Chapter 27

Lotus, Monica, Nicodemus, and Gourd marched down a huge hallway, surrounded by spear-carrying guards. Wreath, still unconscious, floated on a stretcher just behind them. From what Lotus had been able to discern, they were in a palace of some sort. All around them, people (mostly servants, Lotus guessed) stopped to stare as they went by.

At the end of the hallway, they passed through a set of massive doors and then found themselves in a magnificent and grandiose throne room. All around them were servants and attendants, as well as those Lotus pegged as being nobles of some sort.

He and his comrades were marched towards the throne. As they approached, Lotus noticed a young man with a white streak of hair much like himself, sitting on a smaller throne than the one before them, which was huge and clearly the most dominant feature of the room.

Unexpectedly, a loud voice sounded throughout the room from an unknown source.

"All bow before our liege lord," the voice said.

In unison, almost the entire assembly went down to one knee. When Lotus and his companions seemed slow in following suit, one of the guards hissed, "On your knees, *bejkin*!"

Lotus didn't know what the last word meant, but it was obviously an insult of some form. And to emphasize their point, several of the guards struck Lotus and his friends on the back of their legs, making them drop to their knees.

"All hail his name," the unknown voice continued saying. "Eon the Good. Eon the Golden. Eon the God."

EON

Everyone present bowed their heads. Not wanting to get smacked on the noggin, those in Lotus' group did likewise. Out of the corner of his eye, Lotus saw a figure, surrounded by shining light, descend from the heights of the ceiling to the throne. The figure, whom he assumed to be Eon, spoke unexpectedly in a booming voice.

"Which of these cretins makes the claim?" he demanded.

When he failed to reply immediately, a spear poked Lotus in the back. Taking that as his cue, he rose and looked at Eon, but the golden light made it impossible to make out any features.

"I suppose I make the claim," Lotus said.

"Who are you?" Eon asked.

"I have had many names, but I currently answer to the moniker of Ian Lotus."

"Whence came you?"

"I was born on a planet called Earth by its inhabitants."

"How came you into possession of one of my keepsakes, bearing the sigil of my house?"

"I was told by my mother that my father left it for me before he went away. I have carried it with me always."

"The name of your mother?"

"Kelly," Lotus said, after a moment's hesitation. He was so perplexed by what was happening, that for a moment he thought he'd actually forgotten his own mother's name.

"Then, you are mine."

Eon floated down from his throne towards Lotus and halted directly in front of him. The light surrounding Eon diminished, showing Lotus a face startlingly like his

EON

own, although slightly closer to middle age, with the same streak of white hair. He was dressed in what appeared to be richly adorned royal robes and a pendant — much like the one Lotus had worn — hung about his neck. Like Lotus himself, Eon was fairly muscular, and Lotus sensed a power inside the man that went well beyond the mere physical.

Eon hugged Lotus (who was almost too startled to react), and then turned to the royal court.

"Rejoice!" Eon shouted to those assembled, with his arm still around Lotus. "Tonight there will be much feasting. My son — my firstborn — has come home."

Monica glanced at her grandfather and whispered, "Son?"

"I'm as shocked as you are," Nicodemus replied in a low tone.

Lotus was still having trouble processing everything he had heard. "I'm sorry, I don't understand…"

"Then, allow me," Eon said.

He placed a fingertip to Lotus' forehead. Suddenly, Lotus' mind was flooded with thoughts and memories from both the past and the present: his mother…his childhood…playing with his father as a toddler…Eon ruling as a god-king… Lotus almost collapsed under the weight of the images, but was held up by Eon's arm around him.

"What? What?" he mumbled, trying to grasp what he'd just seen.

"I have waited a long time to share those with you," Eon said.

Lotus closed his eyes and shook his head slightly to clear his thoughts.

EON

"Are you really my father?" he asked.

"You already know the answer to that," Eon said. "My blood flows through your veins. Haven't you ever wondered why you were stronger, faster, and more agile than most other men? You are the firstborn and eldest son of Eon. All that you desire shall be yours."

Before Lotus could respond to this, the young man he had seen earlier — the one with a streak of white hair, like he himself had — suddenly appeared next to them.

"Father," the young man said, "why do you lay claim to this...this..." — he looked at Lotus as though he were something floating around in a backed-up toilet — "this mongrel?"

"Nigel," Eon said sternly, "he is your elder brother, and you will treat him with the respect he is due."

A shocked expression took root on Nigel's face. "You honestly expect me to bow to this half-breed?"

"Half-breed?" Lotus repeated angrily. "You arroga—"

"Enough," Eon said in a firm tone. "Nigel, you will follow my edicts or face my wrath. He is elder an—"

"Never!" Nigel declared emphatically. "I will never acknowledge this *pretender* as my superior."

Lotus frowned in thought at the word "pretender." He'd heard it recently, but — with his mind still absorbing the memories he'd received from Eon — he couldn't put it in context. Meanwhile, his "brother" Nigel had continued his tirade.

"I said enough," Eon proclaimed in a no-nonsense tone. He snapped his fingers, and Nigel's voice

EON

died in his throat; he tried to continue speaking, but no words would come out.

Eon turned to Lotus. "Now, I would speak with you, my son. Let us walk."

"What about my friends?" Lotus asked, inclining his heads towards Monica and the others.

Eon glanced at his son's companions, forgotten until now. "They will be cared for — even the injured one."

"Thank you," said Monica.

Eon looked momentarily irritated by her comment, as if she were an insect and her voice a buzzing that had annoyed him. Then he waved his hand, and he and Lotus vanished.

EON

Chapter 28

From Lotus' perspective, the throne room — the entire palace, in fact — seemed to simply vanish. He and Eon were now alone in a beautiful garden full of exotic, alien flora and fauna.

"What?" Lotus said, unable to contain his wonderment at the change in locale. "How…?"

"Mere spatial transposition," Eon said. "Let us walk."

Eon then began strolling leisurely through the garden, with Lotus walking beside him. They sauntered along without haste, and it became clear to Lotus almost immediately, as he watched his companion gently touch a few strikingly colorful flowers, that the garden was of particular significance to his father (although it was difficult to think of this man in those terms).

"This is my special place," Eon finally said. "It is where I come when I want to be alone. You are the first to be invited here."

"Thank you," said Lotus sincerely. "I'm…I'm flattered."

Eon sighed. "I suppose you must have questions for me."

"Yes. I know I asked before, but…are you really my father?"

Eon paused to reflect before he answered. "Long before you were born, I had already ruled Eon — this planet — for an eternity. As time progressed, I grew weary of my duties and responsibilities here. I needed time to refresh my spirit, reanimate my soul."

"A vacation."

EON

"Yes. I chose to visit a small planet whose natives resembled the Eonian race enough that I might pass as one of them. During this period of time, I met a female of whom I became quite fond, and I gave her a child. But when the time came, I had to return to my duties here, and she could not come with me."

"In other words, my mother was just a diversion for you," Lotus muttered, trying hard not to get angry. "A country girl good enough for a roll in the hay, but not sophisticated enough to bring home to meet the family. You never truly loved her."

To his surprise, Eon looked hurt.

"You wrong me," he said. "I am attempting to express emotions and concepts beyond your ken in terms that you may understand. You may not fully appreciate my words because the full range of what I am attempting to convey is not familiar to you, but it is sufficient to say that, in the terms that you mean, I did love your mother. She…rejuvenated me, healed my spirit."

"And yet you left."

"I had no choice."

"And what about me? Did you care for me at all?"

Eon gripped Lotus by the shoulders and looked him squarely in the eye. "You were more important to me than life itself. I loved you like I have loved no other, for you were my firstborn. I looked at you, and saw myself — my past and my future. I loved you more than you can fathom, and should you ever doubt that, look through the memories that I have given you, and you will know. I will always be with you."

Unbidden, a spate of memories suddenly rushed to the forefront of Lotus' brain. Imagery, scenes, and individuals all blitzed his mind, trying to convey something important to him. Slowly, as if through a sieve, the information was sifted until a single element remained, bringing with it a startling revelation.

"That hole in space all those years ago," Lotus said, "the one that poured out that alien data stream. That was you."

"Yes," Eon admitted. "I didn't know exactly where you were, but on certain occasions — particularly when you were under stress — I could sense you."

"Well, the human race was about to be annihilated by the Parsnaak, so I guess you could say I was feeling a little bit of pressure."

"That information was specifically formulated for you — no one else was to be able to truly decipher it."

"Wait a minute." Lotus frowned in thought. "Are you saying that you have the ability to geneticize data? Make it accessible or applicable to only one individual?"

"Of course. However, we didn't really have your full genetic profile, so we extrapolated based on what we knew of human DNA. The purpose was to provide you with the wherewithal to come to us — your family."

"So I was supposed to use the info from that data stream to come here?"

"Yes, but by converting a bit of the technology, you found another application for it."

"The Chronos Ring."

"Yes. You built the weapon that saved your people."

"It's not really a weapon — just a defensive measure," Lotus corrected, then a new thought occurred to him. "Are you angry?"

Eon gave him a perplexed look. "Angry? About what?"

EON

"I used the info you gave me for a purpose you didn't intend."

"You thought that would anger me?" Eon laughed. "On the contrary, I'm proud of your ingenuity. You, my son, are a genius — a credit to your father and his house."

"What about Nigel?" Lotus asked. "He's your son as well. Is he a credit to you?"

Eon was reflective for a moment. "Nigel is the result of a pairing between me and a highborn Eonian noblewoman. He will no doubt be a problem for you, as you have usurped his position. Up until now, he has thought himself my eldest son and my heir. Your presence will change all that, but never fear. He will eventually accept you as his lord, as they all will."

Lotus looked nonplussed. "What do you mean?"

"You are my eldest. By right and by law, you are destined to rule one day."

"But I can't stay," Lotus insisted. "Humanity is in danger. I have to get back."

"All in good time," Eon said with a smile.

"But we don't have time. My people—"

"Are here, on Eon," his father said. "But never fear. If it is your desire to save the Earth-people, you will have the might of all Eon at your beck and call."

"Thank you," Lotus said gratefully.

"No thanks are needed. But it is time we were headed back."

They turned to leave, and found themselves facing Obsidian. Acting on instinct, Lotus immediately pushed his father aside.

Much to Lotus' surprise, the colossal humanoid did nothing. Looking closer, Lotus saw that although

EON

there were many similarities in appearance, this particular individual was *not* Obsidian.

Eon brushed himself off. "Normally it is punishable by death for anyone to profane me with their touch. I can only assume that you had an excellent reason for accosting me."

Lotus pointed to their visitor. "I thought he was going to attack. He looked like another guy who's been trying to kill me."

Eon looked surprised. "An Enforcer? Away from Eon? It is not allowed."

"But that doesn't mean it's impossible."

"You don't understand. Enforcers are genetically bred creatures, unique to our culture. Because of their special characteristics, they are not allowed to transverse space-time without supervision."

"Then what is he doing here? You said no one else was allowed here."

"Again, I am assuming that you understand." Eon looked like someone trying to explain something simple to a child. "An Enforcer is usually a creature of limited will; his desires are those of his master, and in that sense, the Enforcer is not an individual at all. Therefore, even though Vulcan here sometimes accompanies me for protection, for all intents and purposes, I am alone."

"If he's your protection, why didn't he come after me when I pushed you?"

"As I said, Enforcers have limited will. Although you did push me, I did not consider myself threatened by you. And because I did not perceive you as a threat, neither did he. Besides, only I am allowed to shed royal blood. It is death for anyone else to do so."

"I think I understand."

EON

"Go," Eon said in a dreamlike voice that seemed to echo in Lotus' head.

"Go?" Lotus repeated, confused. "Go where?"

Eon looked at him in surprise. "You heard that?"

"Yes," Lotus replied. "Weren't you talking to me?"

The god-king shook his head. "No. That was a mental directive from me to Vulcan. It was not a verbal command."

Glancing around, Lotus noticed that the Enforcer had indeed vanished. "I don't understand."

Lotus' father gave him an appraising glance. "It would seem that you have gifts that go well beyond the norm, even for Eonian royalty. The ability to descry mental communications with Enforcers is a rare talent, with potent implications. It will serve you well in times to come."

"How so?"

"As a member of the Eonian Royal House, you will be given an Enforcer of your own. First, however, you must be trained in the proper control techniques, although – from what I have just observed – that will pose no great obstacle."

"That's all fine, but I'm not sure I have the time. As I said, I'm anxious to return to human space. We only have about a day left."

Eon sighed. "Very well. You will leave as soon as we can prepare a ship for you — a proper ship. In the meantime, we will have a feast in your honor."

EON

Chapter 29

Gourd and Nicodemus were studying what appeared to be an extremely complicated board game. Monica peeked out a window and spied several guards on duty near the door of the guesthouse they were currently in.

"They're still there," she declared.

"Naturally," said Gourd. "Did you expect them to give a party of aliens leave to run amok through their castle?"

"How can you two just sit there?" she asked. "In a few hours, our entire civilization is likely to be destroyed."

"Well, sweetheart, what do you want us to do?" her grandfather asked. "We're at a severe disadvantage here in term of numbers, weapons, and technology."

"What about all those stories you used to tell me when I was a girl, about always having an escape plan? About all the close calls you had?"

"Yeah, but I was younger in those days, and much more stupid," Nicodemus said.

"On the contrary," said an unexpected voice, "I think you're just as stupid now."

They all looked up to see Lotus near the entrance, having entered so quietly that no one had heard him. Smiling in relief at seeing him, his companions suddenly surrounded him, bombarding him with questions.

"What happened?"

"Where have you been?"

"When are we to be released?"

"Slow down," Lotus finally said, raising his hands in an effort to call for order. "Slow down — all of you."

EON

Within seconds, everyone seemed to have calmed down and he went on. "I've been with my...my father. He says that we are to be released, but only after tonight's banquet."

"Banquet?" Monica repeated.

"Yes, he's throwing it in my honor," Lotus stated. "Afterwards he'll give us a ship and the means to cleanse the Chronos Ring of the corrupted code."

Lotus' companions practically cheered at the news.

****

The feast honoring Lotus took place in a banquet hall that could only be described as immense, as was the table that everyone sat at. Sitting in the seat of honor was Lotus. Next to him were his friends: Monica, Nicodemus, and then Gourd. Next to Gourd was an empty chair. Not far away, Nigel glowered at him.

"I wonder who is to sit next to me?" Gourd pondered aloud.

Monica stared at a point beyond him. "At a guess, I'd say your partner in crime."

Gourd turned in the direction indicated and saw Wreath approaching. The media mogul looked extremely fit, and all traces of his burns were gone.

"Good heavens!" Nicodemus cried out. "They've worked a miracle."

Wreath took the empty seat next to Gourd.

"Hello everyone," he said. "Nice to see you all again."

"Holy shit!" Monica said. "We thought you were dead."

EON

"Indeed," Gourd added. "I am surprised you survived your injuries long enough to be treated."

"They have amazingly advanced medical technology here," Wreath said. "Not only did they cure me of my burns, they also cured my illness. I'm fit as a fiddle."

"What's a fiddle?" Monica asked.

"Never mind that," Nicodemus said. "Are we just supposed to forget that you were willing to let the human race be annihilated just to save yourself?"

"Try to understand," Wreath said. "I was mad with fear. I was being struck down with disease in the prime of my life. In short, I wasn't myself. But now that I'm cured, I'm no longer a threat."

"That remains to be seen," Gourd said, plainly skeptical.

"We'll discuss this later," Lotus said. "The food is coming."

At that juncture, servants began bringing out course after course of mouth-watering, succulent dishes that Lotus and his companions had never seen before.

Midway through one of the courses, Wreath signaled to Lotus that he wanted to talk to him. Lotus nodded. Wreath suddenly put down his napkin and rose up.

"Excuse me," he said, "but I think I need to go find the little boys' room."

"I can show you," Lotus chimed in. "I got a tour earlier." (This was, in fact, true, as Lotus had received an impromptu walkthrough prior to rejoining his companions.)

EON

The two men fell into step with each other. As they walked away together, Wreath mumbled under his breath.

"What is it?" Lotus asked.

"Tell you outside," said Wreath.

Lotus nodded and headed towards a set of double-doors that led out onto a colonnade.

"Okay," Lotus said as soon as the doors closed behind them. "What?"

"While they were treating me," Wreath began, "I overheard some things. Things you might want to know."

"Such as?"

"*This.*"

Wreath pointed his index finger at Lotus and a laser beam shot out of it. Lotus took it in the stomach and doubled over. His mouth spasmed wordlessly as he dropped to his knees with a gaping hole in his stomach.

"Sorry about the deception," Wreath said (although not sounding sorry at all), "but nothing comes for free. Sure, their docs fixed me up — even gave me my own built-in laser, plus a few other surprises — but there was a price."

Suddenly the shimmering outline appeared, screeching, "What are you doing, you fool?"

"You said to kill him," Wreath answered. "That was the deal — you fix me up and give me a ship to get back to my own planet, and I help you resolve your issue with Lotus."

"Yes, but you were not supposed to kill him *here*, idiot. I want no evidence to link me back to this pretender's death. Obsidian."

Almost immediately, a spatial rift opened and Obsidian stepped from it onto the colonnade.

EON

"Obsidian," the shimmering shape said, "kindly take this offal to someplace remote and dispose of him."

Lotus, still on his knees, surreptitiously clawed a handful of dirt from the ground. As Obsidian moved toward him, Lotus suddenly flung the dirt into his face. As the Enforcer rubbed his eyes, Lotus unexpectedly rose up, lunged at Wreath and grappled with the media mogul, who was caught off guard. The laser in Wreath's finger went off, sending several beams into the banquet hall. Someone inside screamed.

"Shit!" Wreath blurted out angrily.

He kneed Lotus in his bleeding gut, and Lotus fell to the ground, semi-conscious. He could hear voices as people came out of the banquet hall, but couldn't see anyone yet.

Wreath took a step back, and then zoomed straight into the air as rocket fire burst out from beneath his feet.

As he blacked out, Lotus also saw Obsidian disappear by stepping back into a shining portal.

EON

Chapter 30

Lotus woke to find himself in a large bed, surrounded by his father and friends. Monica, eyes red, leaned over and gave him a huge hug.

"You're alright," she whispered in his ear. Lotus smiled as he hugged her back.

Eventually they separated, at which point Eon asked, "How do you feel?"

"I feel…" Lotus said, focusing on the question and realizing its import, "…fine."

Frowning in confusion, he looked down at his stomach: there was no wound — no sign that he'd ever been injured. Just smooth, unblemished skin.

"The injury has been healed," his father said, "and there will be no scars. Our medics are without peer. I also instructed them to take advantage of the opportunity to make a few changes."

"What kind of changes?" asked Lotus, making no effort to hide his concern.

"Slight augmentations, really," Eon answered. "Nothing of any true significance; do not concern yourself."

Behind Eon, Lotus saw Nicodemus tap his watch and shake his head. Lotus nodded and jumped out of bed.

"We have to go," he said to his father. "We don't have much time."

"But this attack against you cannot go unpunished," Eon insisted. "The culprit must be found and made to pay."

"There's no need to find him," Lotus said. "I know who it is."

EON

****

Nigel was in bed with several beautiful women when the doors to his quarters were thrown open. Lotus entered, followed by his father, his three friends, and several of the Royal Guard. Obsidian, standing nearby, moved as if to protect his prince, but then simply stood still.

Although startled awake, Nigel quickly regained his composure.

"What is the meaning of this intrusion?" he demanded, jumping out of bed as the girls with him slipped demurely from the room. "You have no right—"

"I have every right," his father countered. "I am Eon. Serious charges have been leveled against you, Nigel — accusations that cannot be easily denied."

"By whom? This pretender?" Nigel glared at Lotus.

"'Pretender'!" Lotus repeated. "Now I *know* it's you; you sent that gorilla – as well as Wreath – to kill me." (Mentioning the media mogul brought to mind the fact that, despite an extensive search, the man had yet to be found.)

"What?" Nigel said. "You're mad!"

"No, it's true," Monica stated. "He sent his pet thug to kill us."

"If it is true," Eon said in a dispassionate voice, "it will cost him his life."

For the first time since he'd laid eyes on the younger man, Lotus saw Nigel looking fearful.

"I came here to give you an opportunity to admit your crimes," Eon continued, "and in doing so to claim any possible mercy."

EON

"As I said, this is madness," Nigel insisted.

"Very well," Eon said.

Turning to Lotus, he placed a fingertip to his forehead. Lotus felt something akin to a giant hand sifting through his memories, shuffling through them like a deck of cards until it came up with the specific items it was looking for: his encounters with Obsidian. A second later, the connection broke as Eon turned to face Nigel, growling in anger.

Before his father could say anything, Nigel snapped his fingers, at the same time shouting, "Obsidian, *now*!"

Obsidian rushed over and gripped Eon around the neck, lifting him bodily from the floor and pinning him against the wall. At the same time, another contingent of guards — larger in size than the force that had accompanied Lotus' group to Nigel's quarters — raced into the room, their weapons at the ready. For the moment, everyone held their respective positions, although Nigel's group clearly had the upper hand in terms of sheer numbers.

With a smug look on his face, Nigel turned to Eon, who was still held aloft by Obsidian.

"I know you're probably surprised by this turn of events, Father, but you shouldn't be," he said. "What did you think — that I would willingly give up a throne that is rightfully mine to a half-breed cur? Of course I tried to kill him! From the first moment I found out he existed, I've been tracking him down. Of course, I couldn't be seen to have a hand in his death, so I recruited mercenaries."

"The Parsnaak," Lotus concluded.

175

EON

"Yes," Nigel said with a nod. "They're not too bright, but very effective at killing. And all they wanted in return was a way to overcome that pathetic bit of technology you call the Chronos Ring. Actually, it was a bargain, by my standards."

"You were willing to let billions of innocents be killed just for one man?" Nicodemus asked.

"Not for one man — for a throne!" Nigel announced, eyes gleaming with ambition. "To become the god of Eon!"

"But Eon already has a god," his father said.

"Not for long," Nigel sneered. "Guards, Obsidian — destroy them."

Obsidian began trying to throttle Eon in earnest. At the same time, the guards all began firing — some on behalf of Nigel, others for Eon. While his friends sought cover, Lotus raced up behind Obsidian and jumped on his back. The giant merely seemed to shrug, and Lotus went flying. He slammed into a wall and then fell down onto a wooden table, smashing it.

Eon's golden glow returned as he looked Obsidian in the eye.

"You dare?" he said, as his body became infused with a soft luminescence. "You dare?! I am Eon!"

Struggling to get to his feet, Lotus watched as his father's entire body suddenly turned to a golden liquid, which flowed out of Obsidian's grip and then reformed behind him. Now back in his normal shape, Eon reached down and grabbed the giant by the ankle, and then began slamming him back and forth onto the floor. When Eon released him a few moments later, Obsidian was seemingly unconscious, while much of the tiled floor had been reduced to rubble.

EON

"Guard," Eon said, not forcefully, but projecting in a way that was easily heard.

One of the Royal Guard loyal to Eon ceased firing immediately. Lotus watched in amazement as the man and Eon approached each other amidst a blaze of gunfire.

"Sire?" the guard said, clearly awaiting orders.

"Escort my eldest son back to his own space and time," Eon said.

The guard saluted and then pressed a button on his belt. Almost immediately, a dimensional rift opened next to him. Lotus' companions all rushed towards it and ran through without hesitation. Lotus, bringing up the rear, was about to step into the rift when his father called to him.

"Wait!" Eon shouted, then tossed something to Lotus, who caught it easily. It was his pendant, its broken chain still dangling.

To his surprise, the relic slipped from his grasp and then sealed itself around his neck once more. Lotus smiled; maybe it was merely the comfort that comes with long familiarity, but having the pendant around his neck again brought him a sense of contentment and relaxation that he hadn't realized before.

Lotus was entranced at having unexpectedly received his pendant again and was about to step into the rift when he remembered something crucial.

"I can't leave!" he shouted to his father. "Not without a way to override that corrupt data stream!"

"I am aware of your needs," Eon said. "We have shared minds. Go. You will have the aid you require."

EON

There was so much more he wanted to say, but instead Lotus merely nodded at his father in acknowledgment and stepped into the rift.

EON

Chapter 31

Lotus found himself back on his ship. Already there were his three companions. However, they all looked ill, as if they had eaten something that did not agree with them in the least.

"What is it?" he asked no one in particular.

"Company," Nicodemus replied.

Looking at the viewscreen, Lotus could see a fleet of Parsnaak ships approaching the Chronos Ring, the spheres of which seemed dull and lifeless.

"Oh no," Lotus murmured.

"So what now?" asked Monica.

"Now we start trying to get the Chronos Ring back online," Lotus said.

"Any idea how?" Nicodemus asked.

Lotus shook his head. "No, but my father said he'd send help."

Gourd gave him a skeptical look. "Is it likely to arrive within the next few minutes? Otherwise it will be only a token gesture."

Before Lotus could answer, a dimensional rift opened.

"Thank heavens," Monica said, suddenly feeling more at ease, as was everyone else present.

Their relief, however, was short-lived, as the expected help never appeared. Although the rift stayed open, no one came out of it. After about a minute of tense, silent waiting, everyone was back on edge.

"What happened?" Monica asked. "I thought your father was sending help."

EON

"Maybe there's a glitch," Nicodemus said. "Maybe something is keeping whoever or whatever from coming through."

Lotus, who had been thinking furiously ever since it became clear that the expected aid wasn't going to arrive, shook his head.

"No — there's no glitch," he said, as realization dawned on him. "I think we're looking at this the wrong way. I don't think help is going to come through the rift to us. I think we're supposed to go through it."

"What?" Nicodemus asked, eyebrows raised in surprise.

"That's why it's still open," Lotus said. "It's waiting on us."

"Are you sure?" asked Gourd.

"No, but we're running out of options," Lotus said, glancing at the viewscreen again. The Parsnaak fleet would be in firing range within minutes. Coming to a decision, Lotus said, "You three stay here."

"What are you going to…" Monica began, then started shaking her head. "No. You're not actually going to go in—"

"You bet I am," Lotus said, cutting her off.

"But you don't know where it goes," she said. "You're doing this based on a guess."

"If I'm wrong, it won't be the worst guess I've ever made," he said. Then, acting on impulse, he reached for a small device on a nearby console and held it up for her to see. "But if it makes you feel any better, I'll wear a comm relay."

With that, he fitted the device in his ear, and then headed for the rift.

EON

"Wait!" Monica yelled. She ran over and, to Lotus' surprise, gave him a deep, passionate kiss.

"Wow," he said when she pulled back a moment later. "What was that for — luck?"

"The shape of things to come," she corrected him. "An incentive not to get killed."

Lotus smiled, gave her a wink, and then stepped through the rift.

EON

Chapter 32

Lotus stepped out of the rift and into a large room that he didn't immediately recognize, although something about it was definitely familiar. All around him was lots of high-tech equipment: computer banks, monitors, and so on. A sense of déjà vu descended on him as he looked around his new environs, growing in intensity until — with a jolt — he realized where he was.

Lotus started laughing.

"Ian," Monica's voiced piped in his ear. "Is everything okay?"

"Everything's fine."

"Great. We were worried for a moment that you might have ended up some place out of range of the comm system. Then we heard you laughing. Do you know where you are?"

"Yes," he said. "I'm on — actually *in* — the primary site of the Chronos Ring! The control sphere."

It had been decades since he'd last set foot in this place (although he was actually only in the front compartment). It hadn't changed at all, nor was there any reason it should have. Everything dealing with the Ring was automated. He'd seen to that when he set it up. The only reason a person ever needed to be here…

With that thought, Lotus suddenly stopped reminiscing and focused on the business at hand. His father had promised help, but instead had sent him here. *Why? Was there something he was supposed to do?*

Lotus dashed over to one of the computer consoles. Looking at a nearby monitor, he saw a display indicating the interference with the Ring's function. He didn't know what Eon had planned, but rather than just

EON

sit idle like a damsel in a tower waiting to be rescued, he decided to see what — if anything — he could do. He began typing on the keyboard of one of the consoles, examining the profile of the corrupt data, trying to look for an angle that would let him undermine it.

Without warning, a glut of information once again surged through his mind — this time scientific in nature: data, coding, formulas, etc. Moreover, the material unfolded in such a way that he immediately understood it.

Lotus laughed again as — now armed with the necessary knowledge — he began inputting the requisite information into the primary site.

"What's going on over there?" Nicodemus' voice said through the comm. "What's happening?"

"Nothing," Lotus said. "I think everything's under control now."

"It better be," Nicodemus practically growled. "The Parsnaak are damn near on top of us."

Lotus didn't respond, preferring to focus on the task before him (although he did spare a few seconds to bring up an image of the approaching invasion fleet on one of the large monitors). For the next minute, he was completely locked in on returning the Chronos Ring to normal operation.

From all indications, it was working; the Ring was slowly coming back online as he worked to cut off the disruptive flow of data. He was just a few excited keyboard clicks away from finishing when something like a sledgehammer clubbed him on the side of the head and sent him reeling.

Lotus staggered like a drunk for a few steps and then collapsed to the floor with pain exploding in his skull. He tried to figure out what had happened — see what was going on — but his vision was blurred. He shook his head in an attempt to clear it, but everything was still hazy. He struggled up to his hands and knees, only to receive a kick in the side that he was positive cracked a few ribs as it sent him flying backwards until he hit a wall with a bone-jarring smack.

Looking around, his vision seemed to be returning to normal, although he could still only make out fuzzy shapes. That said, one of those shapes appeared to move in his direction. At the same time, he heard an enraged voice shouting.

"Kill him, Obsidian!" said the voice. "Kill the pretender!"

Nigel...

Now Lotus knew what had happened. He had been so focused on fixing the Chronos Ring, so intense was his concentration, that he hadn't even realized that he was no longer alone. Nigel (and clearly Obsidian) had joined him aboard the sphere. Hell, for all he knew, they may have already been there when he arrived.

Trying to ignore the pain in his side and his head, Lotus scrambled along on all fours as best he could, struggling to buy time while he figured something out. Thankfully, his vision came back into focus. Unfortunately, it did him little good as something like a boulder smashed down on his back, collapsing him to the floor.

It didn't take a lot of imagination on Lotus' part to figure out that Obsidian had basically stepped on him. Now the giant was slowly applying pressure, apparently intent on squashing Lotus like a bug. Lotus struggled to get up, but did little more than make wriggling motions as the weight on his back started to increase painfully.

EON

"Wait!" Nigel suddenly shouted. "Don't kill him yet. Bring him here."

Without preamble, Lotus found himself grabbed by the scruff of the neck and hoisted up into the air. He was then carried over to Nigel, who stood in front of the console Lotus had been working at just moments ago with a lasergun in his hand. Obsidian, gripping Lotus on either side and pinning his arms, stood him up before Nigel. The Eonian prince stared at Lotus with pure menace in his eyes.

"You've ruined everything!" he screamed in Lotus' face. "Taken everything from me! I'm a vagabond now, fleeing my father's justice. My titles, my positions, my powers…all gone because of you."

Nigel punched Lotus in the stomach, holding nothing back. It was all Lotus could do not to retch. As it was, the only reason he remained on his feet was because Obsidian was holding him up.

"Well," Nigel continued, "since you've taken everything from me, I feel compelled to return the favor."

Nigel glanced at the monitor, where the Parsnaak fleet could be seen continuing its approach.

"In minutes," Nigel said, "the Parsnaak will be in position to destroy the Ring. They'll blast it apart, sphere by sphere, while at the same time sending regiments to conquer every system occupied by the human race. Humanity will be Parsnaak slaves for the rest of eternity. And you'll get to watch how it begins."

"Don't!" Lotus screamed. "Don't do this! The rest of humanity doesn't deserve what's going to happen. They haven't done anything to you. Just take your pound of flesh from me and leave everyone else alone. Don't punish *them* — punish *me*."

EON

"But this *is* to punish you," Nigel said. "Their pain is your pain. Even I can see that. But don't worry, you won't live to see my entire prediction come true about humanity's future slavery — just the beginning of it."

Nigel turned away and watched the invasion fleet approach. Lotus, held immobile in Obsidian's grip, wanted to scream. *He had been so close!* Just a few keystrokes more and it would have been done — the Ring would have been back online. *If only he could reach the console...*

An idea suddenly occurred to him. It was a small chance — a tiny window of opportunity — and he didn't have much time, but it was better than nothing. Lotus took a deep breath and concentrated.

Thankfully, Nigel seemed to be eagerly watching the monitor rather than paying attention to his captive; he seemed more interested in witnessing the anticipated destruction of the Ring (and perhaps the ensuing slaughter and enslavement of the human race). Any second now, the Parsnaak fleet would begin firing, and the Eonian prince was practically rubbing his hands together with glee.

All of a sudden, the primary site began to shudder, and the sounds of dormant machinery suddenly shifting into operation permeated the sphere. Nigel looked around in surprise, trying to assess what was happening, and then the truth dawned on him: the primary site was coming back online. Lotus was unable to keep a smile of his face as he noticed, via the monitor, that all of the other spheres were likewise becoming functional again. In short, the Ring was coming back online.

EON

Nigel spun towards Lotus, who was just a little slow in removing the grin from his face.

"What did you do?" Nigel demanded, walking towards him. He pointed his lasergun at Lotus' forehead. "What did you do?!"

Lotus didn't say anything, which only incensed Nigel even more.

"Kill him," Nigel said to Obsidian. "But slowly. Painfully."

However, before the colossus could carry out the order, the primary site shook again, this time so violently that Nigel was thrown to the floor and even Obsidian had to release his grip on Lotus in order to maintain his balance.

Once free, Lotus wasted no time, running at breakneck speed towards the rear area of the sphere, with shots from Nigel's weapon peppering the air around him. Diving behind some crates, Lotus hugged the wall and scampered down its length, hoping to find better cover. He eventually settled in behind a tarp-covered piece of machinery.

"You better leave if you want to live," Lotus shouted, just as the sphere experienced another violent jolt.

Nigel laughed. "Your threats are worse than idle. You seem to forget who has the weapons here, as well as the advantage of numbers."

"No, I didn't," Lotus replied, still continuing to move. "You've miscounted."

"Oh? How so?"

"When I brought the Ring back online, I also had it scan you and your buddy. I had it designate your bio-signatures as enemies of humanity. In short, every sphere

EON

of the Ring is going to be focused on destroying this site within minutes."

"You lie!" Nigel said fiercely.

"Do I? Stick around and find out. Every shudder you feel is another part of the Ring firing on our location."

As if to lend truth to Lotus' words, tremors again shook the sphere. When they ended, there were a few moments of tense silence. Suddenly, there was a groan of immense frustration from Nigel, accompanied by a barrage of random shots into the rear part of the sphere. (None of which, thankfully, came close to hitting Lotus.) A few moments later, he thought he detected a flash of light, and then he sensed more than saw that he was alone.

Lotus let out a sigh of relief. *That had been entirely too close.* Standing up, he headed back towards the front of the sphere. Once there, he did a quick check of the computer systems and was happy to see that the Ring appeared to be functioning normally. On the monitor, he saw the Parsnaak fleet in full retreat, with one ship at the rear — perhaps a little slower than the others — getting blasted apart by several Ring spheres.

Lotus was about to congratulate himself on a job well done when a dimensional rift opened near him. Of course — it was his way back to the ship with his friends. He was about to head for it when he saw an immense foot step out of it.

Obsidian...

It looked as though Nigel was calling his bluff. More out of reflex than design, Lotus backpedaled, retreating from the gargantuan body that was coming out of the rift. At that moment, the sphere shook again, causing him to lose his balance. He went down backwards, smacking the base of his skull on something (probably some piece of machinery) before flopping to the floor in a daze.

His eyes fluttered and he fought to stay conscious, but it was the second blow he'd taken to the noggin in a very short period of time. He'd be lucky if he didn't have a concussion.

Lotus tried to stand — to sit up — but didn't seem to have control of his motor functions. Hell, simply lying on the floor seemed to take a massive amount of effort. He looked in the direction of the rift, trying to see where Obsidian was. His eyes, however, refused to focus and darkness began to creep in at the edge of his vision. It wasn't until he saw two mammoth-sized feet just inches from his head that he realized how close the giant was. He swung feebly at his adversary, but by then it was too late.

Lotus passed out as a pair of enormous hands reached down and grabbed him.

EON

Chapter 33

For the second time in recent memory, Lotus came to in a strange bed. From the odd constriction around his temples, he knew that his head was bandaged — and the same was true of his chest. He was in a large room, but it didn't have the antiseptic feel of a hospital environment: there was carpet on the floor, some shelves full of books, and a couple of chairs that actually looked comfortable to sit in.

Lotus threw back the covers, got out of bed, and stretched. There was a dull ache in his head and his torso, but — based on past experience — he didn't feel that there was any permanent damage to anything. He stepped over to a large window covered by drapes and was about to peek out when he heard the door open.

"Oh, you're awake," said a perky young blonde in a nurse's uniform. "Just a moment."

She backed out and closed the door before Lotus could say anything. He walked to the door and was about to grab the handle when it opened and Nicodemus stepped in.

"Awake at last," Nicodemus said. "It's about time."

"How long was I out?" Lotus asked.

"About a day-and-a-half. You were pretty banged up, but I see you heal now just as quickly as you did in the old days. And now I know why."

"Yeah," Lotus said. "About that..."

"Don't worry," Nicodemus assured him. "Your secret is safe with us. Even Gourd has taken a sacred vow of the yellow calf—"

"Yallo-cafalla," Lotus corrected.

EON

"Yeah, that. He said you'd understand what it meant."

"It's the strongest oath a Corsian can make."

"So I've been told. That being the case, it's probably safe to assume he won't be spilling the beans about you any time soon."

"Good to know," Lotus said. "Where is he, by the way?"

"He and Monica went to run some errands. We're a little low on provisions."

"Where exactly are we?"

Nicodemus smiled. "A little hideaway that not many people know about."

"One of the perks of being the head of Galactic Intel, I suppose, is having a lot of black ops sites that are off the books."

"Rank has its privileges," the older man conceded. "Anyway, since you seem to be on the path to recovery, maybe now I can finally get answers to some questions."

"Such as?"

"What the hell happened on the primary site?"

Lotus hesitated for a moment, his natural reticence to sharing information coming to the fore. Then he mentally shrugged. He'd spent a lifetime — several, in fact — carrying far too many secrets. Nick had been along for much of the recent ride; it didn't make sense to cut him off now.

Decision made, he gave Nicodemus a swift account of what had happened. Unsurprisingly, it was not a long story (especially when considering that everything had unfolded in just a few minutes' time). When he was done, the older man studied him for a moment.

EON

"So Nigel didn't know about your telekinesis?" Nicodemus asked, almost unbelievingly.

"Apparently not, despite all the effort he put into tracking me down," Lotus said. "Or if he did know, it slipped his mind in the heat of the moment. Regardless, I just used that ability to hit the last few keys and reactivate the Ring while Obsidian was holding me."

"And then you bluffed him? Made him think the Ring was programmed to attack him?"

"Yeah," Lotus said. "One of the things Nigel's corrupted data stream did was take the engines of the primary site offline. When I activated everything again, apparently the engines had trouble firing up — they had the whole place shaking like we were on an earthquake fault line. I just used what was happening to support an impromptu fiction about what I'd done."

"But how did you know he'd fall for it?"

"I didn't, but I've met men like him before — arrogant, and with an elevated perception of their own self-importance. I trusted that self-preservation would rank very high on his to-do list."

"And it looks like you were right."

"Maybe only half-right, since he called my bluff at the end and sent Obsidian to finish me off," Lotus said. "Which begs the question — how did you guys get me away from him?"

Nicodemus shook his head in confusion. "We never did. After you brought the Ring back online, we just watched it run the Parsnaak fleet off and waited for you to return."

"Huh?" Lotus frowned. "But if you and the others didn't come get me, how did I get back to you?"

EON

"You mean you don't know?" Nicodemus asked, his eyebrows going up in surprise.

"No," Lotus said, shaking his head.

"Hmmm," Nicodemus said. "Come with me."

He stepped over to the door with Lotus on his heels, and then opened it. On the other side was a long, broad hallway, and standing directly across from the door was a familiar-looking giant.

Lotus sucked in a harsh breath, his body getting ready to shift into action, and then he realized that the giant hadn't moved. More to the point, as he looked more closely, he realized that the colossus facing them wasn't Obsidian. It was another Enforcer.

"That's how you got back to us," Nicodemus said, pointing at the massive figure.

Lotus closed the door, then let out a ragged breath and said, "I don't understand…"

"Neither do any of us," Nicodemus said. "All we know is that a rift opened up on the ship, and we initially thought it was you coming back. But it turned out to be that fellow" — he pointed at the door — "carrying you, unconscious. He didn't attack and didn't look like he was going to go anywhere, so we got the hell out of there, taking him with us."

"And you brought him here?"

"No, he came along on his own, going wherever you went. And it's not like anyone could stop him. I mean, come on — you've seen those things in action. All I would have done was gotten good people killed if I tried to control him. Plus, all he's done is follow you around like a puppy. He's been parked across that hall since we brought you here."

EON

Lotus merely nodded in acknowledgment, reflecting back as Nicodemus spoke. It was clear to him now that it was this new Enforcer he'd seen coming through the rift that last time on the primary site, not Obsidian.

Taking Lotus' silence for exhaustion, Nicodemus excused himself.

"Just understand that Monica will be knocking down your door the second she gets back and finds out you're awake," the older man said as he was leaving.

"Understood," Lotus said, then closed the door behind his departing visitor.

As he turned around, Lotus noticed a golden pinprick of light beginning to shine in the center of the room. As he watched, it grew larger and brighter; then, without warning, the glow diminished and the light coalesced into the features of his father.

"I am sorry our reunion was so brief," Eon said, "but you understand now the pressures I face. I have sent you Cerulean to serve you and yours. He is an Enforcer of the first rank, and will defy even me to carry out your orders. I wish you much success in the future, and look forward to the day we shall meet again. Until then, goodbye, my son."

As Eon's face slowly faded, Lotus whispered, "Goodbye, Father. And thank you."

THE END

EON

Thank you for purchasing this book! If you enjoyed it, please feel free to leave a review on the site from which it was purchased.

Also, if you would like to be notified when I release new books, please subscribe to my mailing list via the following link: http://eepurl.com/b0-hBL

Finally, for those who may be interested, I have included my blog info: http://earlehardman.blogspot.com/

BLAISDELL MEMORIAL LIBRARY
NOTTINGHAM, NH 03290-0115
WITHDRAWN

Made in the USA
Middletown, DE
12 August 2016